WHEN LAVENDER BLOOMS AGAIN

A World War II Historical Romance of Love & Resistance

EVA LYNDALE

WHEN LAVENDER BLOOMS AGAIN

For my family—whose boundless love and support fill every page with light.

CONTENTS

PROLOGUE: WHEN LAVENDER BLOOMED

The scent of lavender hung heavy in the morning air, sweet and clean and eternal. Marguerite Dubois moved through the purple rows with the practiced rhythm of someone born to this work, her grandmother's curved serpe catching the early light as she cut the fragrant stems. Behind her, the old wicker baskets filled steadily with the harvest that would sustain them through another year.

"Not too low," her mother Amélie called from the next row, her voice carrying the gentle authority of a woman who had learned this craft from her own mother-in-law forty years ago. "Leave enough stem for next year's growth."

Twenty-two-year-old Marguerite smiled at the familiar reminder. She had been harvesting lavender since she was old enough to hold a knife, had learned the ancient rhythms of this work before she could properly read. But Amélie never tired of passing on the small wisdoms that made the difference between a good harvest and a great one.

The war felt very distant on mornings like this.

France had fallen three weeks ago—that was the stark reality everyone in the village had been forced to accept. The government had fled to Vichy, the Germans were in Paris, and the radio brought news of occupation and armistice and collaboration. But here in Provence, in these fields that had been tended by Dubois hands for three generations, the ancient cycles continued unchanged.

Henri emerged from the farmhouse carrying a wooden tray laden with coffee and fresh bread, walking with the slight limp that was his only visible reminder of the last war. At fifty-three, Marguerite's father had the weathered look of a man who had spent his life working this difficult soil, but his eyes were peaceful as he surveyed his family and his land.

"Rest," he called, settling the tray on the stone wall that separated the lavender fields from the farmyard. "The lavender isn't going anywhere."

Fifteen-year-old Pierre straightened from his work with obvious relief, wiping sweat from his forehead with the back of his hand. He was growing fast, all knees and elbows and earnest enthusiasm, still young enough to find the repetitive work of harvest tedious but old enough to understand its importance.

"Papa," he said, settling onto the wall beside his father, "Monsieur Beaumont says the Germans will be here by autumn. He says they'll want to requisition our harvest."

Henri's expression grew thoughtful as he poured coffee from the blue enamel pot that had been his wedding gift to Amélie. "Monsieur Beaumont talks too much and thinks too little," he said finally. "The Germans want order, not chaos. They have no interest in destroying what feeds people."

Marguerite accepted her cup of coffee—real coffee, still available in these last precious weeks before shortages would become a way of life —and studied her father's face. Henri had fought at Verdun, had seen what happened when civilized nations abandoned the pretense of civilization. But he was also a practical man who understood that worry was a luxury farmers could not afford.

"The harvest will be good this year," Amélie said, settling beside her husband with the natural grace of a woman comfortable in her own skin. At forty-eight, she retained the beauty that had attracted Henri when she was the village schoolteacher and he was a young farmer trying to rebuild his father's land after the last war.

"The best in years," Henri agreed, looking out over the purple-silver sea of lavender that stretched across the hillside. "The spring rains were perfect, the summer heat just right. The distillery will work overtime to process it all."

Pierre picked up a lavender stem and twirled it between his fingers, releasing its fragrance into the warm air. "Will we still be able to sell it? With the war and everything?"

"People will always need lavender oil," Marguerite said confidently. "For soap, for medicine, for perfume. Wars come and go, but lavender is forever."

It was a family saying, passed down from Marguerite's great-grandmother, who had planted the first fields in these hills when the Franco-Prussian War was reshaping Europe. Each generation had faced its own crises—drought and disease, market collapse and political upheaval—but the lavender had endured.

The morning stretched ahead of them, filled with the simple satisfactions of work that connected them to the land and to each other. Marguerite found herself memorizing the scene without quite understanding why—the way the light fell across her mother's dark hair, the sound of Pierre's laughter as he told some elaborate story about the village boys, the comfortable weight of her father's presence as he planned the afternoon's work.

This was peace. This was home. This was the life they had built together through patience and hard work and the kind of love that didn't need words to express itself.

The war might be reshaping the world beyond these hills, but here in their lavender fields, time moved to older rhythms. The sun rose and set, the seasons turned, the harvest came and went according to patterns that had been established long before nations and armies had any meaning.

"Back to work," Henri said finally, rising and stretching muscles that had been bent to this labor for more than thirty years. "The afternoon will be hot, and we want to finish the east field before the heat becomes unbearable."

They returned to their work with the easy coordination of people who had been harvesting together for years. The baskets filled steadily with purple-gray stems that would soon be transformed into the essential oil that was their livelihood and their legacy.

Marguerite paused once more to look back at the farmhouse—the honey-colored stone walls that had sheltered her family for generations, the red tile roof that had weathered countless storms, the ancient oak tree that provided shade for the kitchen courtyard. Everything looked exactly as it always had, peaceful and permanent and secure.

She couldn't know that this would be the last normal harvest for four years. Couldn't know that by next summer, her father would be in hiding and her mother would be dead and she herself would be calculating survival in terms of requisitioned livestock and disappeared neighbors.

All she knew was the weight of the serpe in her hand, the fragrance of lavender in the morning air, and the deep contentment that came from working land that had been shaped by love across generations.

The war would come to their hills soon enough. But for now, in this perfect moment suspended between the innocence of the past and the uncertainty of the future, there was only this—the eternal rhythm of harvest, the unbreakable bonds of family, and the promise that lavender would bloom again no matter what storms might come.

In her basket, the purple stems released their fragrance into the warming air, carrying with them the essence of a life that was about to change forever but would never be entirely lost.

The scent of home. The scent of hope. The scent of everything worth fighting to preserve.

❧

THE LAVENDER HARVEST

AUGUST 1942

The lavender sang in the morning wind, but Marguerite Dubois heard only the arithmetic of survival.

Two years of occupation had taught her to calculate in portions and probabilities: one-quarter of their harvest claimed by German requisitions, half their chickens gone to feed the garrison at Manosque, seventeen villagers disappeared into the night and fog of Nazi justice. Numbers were safer than names, statistics less painful than faces.

She paused in her cutting, the curved blade of her grandmother's serpe heavy in her hand, and watched the sun creep across the valley. At twenty-four, she'd inherited her mother's careful beauty and her father's stubborn jaw, though both features had sharpened under rationing's slow erosion. The lavender stretched before her in perfect rows, purple waves that had once meant prosperity and now meant survival—if they could hide enough oil from German auditors, if the weather held, if a thousand other variables aligned.

"You're thinking too loud," her father said, appearing between the rows with his distinctive limp—Verdun's permanent souvenir. Henri

Dubois moved through his fields like a man reading scripture, each plant a verse in the gospel of endurance. "The plants can hear worry. Makes the oil bitter."

"Then this year's harvest will taste of wormwood." But she smiled, resuming her cutting. It was an old game between them, her mother's whimsy filtered through their practical natures.

"Your mother never worried," Henri said, though they both knew it for a lie. Amélie Dubois had worried beautifully, transforming anxiety into action, fear into quiet resistance. Even cancer hadn't stopped her worrying—she'd planned her own funeral between morphine doses, ensuring her family would grieve efficiently.

"Maman worried differently," Marguerite corrected. "With purpose."

"Everything she did had purpose." Henri's voice carried the particular softness reserved for the year-dead. "Including leaving us to manage alone."

They worked in companionable silence, the rhythm of harvest as familiar as breath. Cut low but not too low, bundle quickly before the sun climbed too high, leave enough stem for the plant's survival. The metaphor wasn't lost on either of them—France itself being harvested, carefully, sustainably, by occupiers who planned a thousand-year Reich.

"Marguerite!" Pierre's voice cracked across the field—seventeen years old and caught between boy and man, his voice betraying him at crucial moments. "They're coming! Three trucks from the village!"

The serpe stilled in her hand. Three trucks meant hunger—German efficiency clearing shelves that were already bare. She and Henri exchanged glances, a conversation in microseconds: hide what they could, surrender what they must, survive another day.

"The new cache?" she asked.

"Behind the old olive press. Pierre knows." Henri was already moving, his limp more pronounced with urgency. "Twenty liters of oil, some preserved vegetables. Not much, but—"

"But enough to mean prison if discovered." She gathered the morning's cutting, mind racing through their defensive lies. The Germans had grown suspicious after too many "poor harvests" and "unfortunate blights." Even occupiers could count, and the Dubois farm's mathematics had stopped adding up.

Pierre met them at the tool shed, his face flushed with more than exertion. At seventeen, he'd inherited their mother's fine features and their father's dangerous idealism. The combination worried Marguerite more than German requisitions.

"Sergeant Mueller says the Wehrmacht are with them," Pierre reported, breathless. "Looking for someone specific."

Mueller—they recognized the name. Not the worst of the German garrison, but far from the best. He spoke functional French and had mentioned a wife in Hamburg, small humanizations that made his authority no less absolute.

"Who?" Henri asked.

"Don't know. But they're asking about aircraft." Pierre's eyes held dangerous excitement. "Allied aircraft, imagine!"

"Imagine them elsewhere," Henri said sharply. "We have enough troubles without borrowing more."

They dispersed to their tasks—Henri to greet their unwelcome visitors with calculated submission, Pierre to ensure their hidden stores remained so, Marguerite to continue the harvest as if German trucks were no more concerning than morning mist. Performance as survival, each playing their assigned role.

The trucks growled into their courtyard, disgorging soldiers with the bored efficiency of experience. Marguerite recognized Mueller immediately—stocky, graying, the kind of man who'd been a factory foreman before the war made him temporary master of a French valley.

"Herr Dubois," Mueller called, not quite managing the French 'r'. "Inspection time again. You know the procedure."

"Of course, Sergeant." Henri's voice held just the right blend of resignation and respect. "How can we assist the Reich today?"

"By having your quota ready. Forty kilos of lavender oil, twenty of wheat, whatever vegetables you've managed." Mueller consulted a leather-bound ledger. "The Reich requires contribution from all citizens."

"The oil..." Henri spread his hands in a gesture perfected over three years. "The late frost damaged our harvest severely. We have perhaps ten kilos—"

"Twenty is the requirement." Mueller's tone suggested this was not a negotiation. "Find it."

Marguerite continued cutting lavender, letting her movements slow to suggest simple rural stupidity. But her ears tracked every sound —boots on gravel, truck doors slamming, the particular clink of weapons being adjusted. More activity than a standard requisition required.

"You, girl!" A voice in accented French. One of Mueller's subordinates, young and eager to prove himself. "What do you know about aircraft?"

She straightened slowly, blinking as if confused by the question. "Aircraft, monsieur?"

"Don't play stupid. Planes. Flying machines. Have you seen any crash nearby?"

"I see them often." She gestured vaguely skyward. "They make lines in the sky. Sometimes they fight, like dancing birds."

The soldier's face darkened at her apparent simplicity. "Recently. Low-flying aircraft. Crashed aircraft. Two days ago."

"Oh." She pretended to think, serpe hanging loose in her hand. "Two days ago, perhaps? There was noise to the east, toward the mountains. But Papa says it's not our business to wonder about such things."

"Your Papa is wise." Mueller had approached, his older authority checking his subordinate's enthusiasm. "But if you see anything unusual—strangers, injured men—it becomes your business to report it. Understood?"

"Yes, Sergeant." She bobbed her head, the picture of rural compliance. "Should I stop my work to watch for such things?"

"Don't be clever, girl. It doesn't suit you." But Mueller's attention had already shifted, scanning their property with professional assessment. "Brunner, check the outbuildings. Weiss, the house. Standard search."

Marguerite's hands resumed cutting, but her mind raced. A search meant they suspected something specific. The hidden oil would survive—Pierre was clever about concealment. But if they'd truly heard about downed airmen...

She thought of the Tessier family, disappeared six months ago for the crime of possessing a radio. Of Dr. Bernard's assistant, shot for treating a wounded resistant. The arithmetic of resistance was brutal: help one enemy of the Reich, risk everything.

The search proceeded with German thoroughness. They found the official stores, counted and catalogued for requisition. They missed the cache, Pierre's cleverness holding against routine inspection. But as the soldiers prepared to leave, Mueller paused near Marguerite's position.

"Two days ago, you said. The noise to the east."

"Perhaps. Time moves strangely during harvest." She kept her eyes on her work. "Was it important?"

"A British bomber was shot down. Four engines, ten crew. We've found eight bodies." His pale eyes studied her face. "The other two might be injured, seeking help. It would be... unfortunate if someone aided enemies of the Reich."

"Very unfortunate," she agreed, not looking up. "We have enough misfortune already."

"Yes. Your mother's death. Your brother's youth. Your father's injury." Mueller counted their vulnerabilities like rosary beads. "Much to lose for a family already diminished."

The threat hung between them, precise as a blade. Then he turned away, calling his men to order. The trucks departed in clouds of dust and diesel, leaving the farm poorer but intact.

"Well?" Henri asked when they regrouped.

"They're hunting airmen. British bomber crew." Marguerite set down her basket, hands trembling slightly. "Two unaccounted for."

"Not our concern," Henri said firmly. "We can't save every—"

A sound cut him off. Faint but unmistakable—a groan of pain from the direction of the old goat shed.

They froze, three generations of Dubois caught between conscience and survival. The shed had been empty for two years, since they'd sold the goats to pay taxes. No reason for sounds to emerge from abandoned spaces.

"It's nothing," Henri said. "Old wood settling."

Another groan, more distinct. Human pain given voice.

"Papa," Pierre said quietly. "We can't just—"

"We can't anything. Whatever you're thinking, stop." Henri's face had gone stern, the expression that had carried him through one war and into another. "We check our stored feed. If we happen to find injured wildlife, we make appropriate decisions. But we go armed, and we go careful."

They approached the shed like soldiers, which in a way they'd all become. Henri carried his ancient hunting rifle, Marguerite a pitch-fork, Pierre a harvesting knife. The door hung askew on rusted hinges, interior dim with years of dust.

The British airman lay in the far corner, flight suit torn and blood-ied, leg bent at an angle that made Marguerite's stomach turn. Young—perhaps twenty-five, perhaps younger—with sandy hair and the kind of square jaw that suggested stubbornness as a genetic trait. Blood seeped from a dangerously infected gash along his side, the wound's edges already showing signs of poisoning. His eyes flickered open at their approach, blue and fevered and absolutely foreign.

"Please," he whispered in accented French. "S'il vous plaît. Je suis..."

"We know what you are," Henri interrupted. "The question is what to do with you."

"Papa, he's dying," Pierre protested. "Look at him!"

Marguerite was looking. Seeing not just the injured airman but the cascade of consequences his presence initiated. Hiding him meant death if discovered. Turning him in meant collaboration with occu-piers. Leaving him to die meant living with cowardice. The arithmetic offered no clean solutions.

"Can you walk?" she asked in careful English, learned from her mother who'd believed languages were windows to wider worlds.

Surprise flickered across his features. "You speak... yes, I mean, no. Leg's buggered. Broken when I landed." His voice carried British understatement despite obvious agony. "James Crawford, RAF. I'm sorry to involve you. I'll leave if—"

"You'll die if you leave." She crouched beside him, assessing damage with hands made practical by farm life. "How long have you been here?"

"Since last night. Crawled here after landing. My radio operator..." His face tightened. "Didn't make it out."

"The Germans found eight bodies," Henri said in French. "You're one of two they're hunting."

"Then I need to move. Can't bring trouble to—" James tried to sit up, gasped, fell back. "Bloody hell. Sorry. Language."

"Your language is the least of our problems." Marguerite switched to French for her father. "We can't move him like this. The leg needs setting, the wounds cleaning. He needs time."

"Time we don't have. The Germans—"

"Won't return immediately. They've filled their quotas." She met her father's eyes. "Maman would have helped him."

"Your mother would have been practical about risks."

"Maman hid three Jewish children in 1941," Pierre said quietly. "I helped her. The Kellerman children. She found them passage to Switzerland through the church network. She said saving lives was the only mathematics that mattered."

The revelation landed like a blow. Henri stared at his son, then at Marguerite, who was equally stunned. Their careful mother, keeping secrets even from family.

"When?" Henri asked finally.

"March through May. She said you had enough burdens carrying this farm and us. But I think she'd want us to help him."

Henri closed his eyes, communing with his dead wife's ghost. When he opened them, resignation had replaced resistance. "One week. We hide him one week while he heals enough to travel. Then he goes."

"Papa—"

"One week, Marguerite. After that, we're all at risk." He turned to James, switching to careful English. "You understand? Seven days, then you must go."

"I understand. And thank you. I know the risk—"

"No, you don't. But you will." Henri studied him with eyes that had seen too much. "Can you stay quiet? When patrols come, when dogs search, when fear makes you want to cry out—can you be silent?"

"I can be whatever keeps you safe."

"We'll see." Henri turned away. "Pierre, get medical supplies. Marguerite, prepare the hidden space in the loft. I'll watch for patrols. And all of us—we tell no one. Not friends, not God himself. This secret stays or we all hang."

They scattered to their tasks, the rhythm of crisis as familiar as harvest. Marguerite climbed to the shed's loft, clearing years of detritus to reveal the hidden space her grandfather had built during the last war. Some paranoia transcended generations.

Below, James Crawford watched her work, fever-bright eyes tracking her movements. "I'm sorry," he said again. "For bringing this danger."

"Danger was already here," she replied, spreading straw to create a pallet. "You're just making it specific."

"Very French of you. Finding philosophy in disaster."

"Very British of you, apologizing while bleeding." She descended the ladder carefully. "We need to move you up before treating the leg. Can you manage?"

What followed was controlled agony. James bit through a leather strap to muffle screams as they maneuvered him up the ladder. His leg was indeed broken, bone grinding against bone with each movement. By the time they had him settled in the hidden space, all three were drenched in sweat.

"Now the pleasant part," Marguerite said, preparing to set the bone. "Pierre, hold him down. Papa, be ready with the splint."

"Wait." James gasped, reaching for her hand. "If I pass out—if I die —tell my family I was thinking of them. Sarah especially. My sister. She worries."

"Tell her yourself when you get home." She gripped his hand briefly, then nodded to Pierre. "Now."

The bone set with a wet snap that made Pierre gag. James didn't scream—couldn't, with the leather between his teeth—but his body convulsed with pain. Then merciful unconsciousness claimed him.

They worked quickly after that, cleaning wounds, binding the leg, making him as comfortable as possible in the cramped space. The infected gash required careful attention—Marguerite cleaned it thoroughly, though she worried about blood poisoning without proper medicine. The burns on his hands were concerning as well, but the gash was the immediate threat.

When James finally regained consciousness, his fever-bright eyes found Marguerite's face. "You're an angel," he whispered, voice thick with pain and gratitude. "You've saved my life, Marguerite Dubois."

"No angels," she replied practically, checking his temperature with the back of her hand. "Just farmers with more conscience than sense."

"He'll need constant care," Marguerite said as they finished. "Fever, infection, the leg—someone must check every few hours."

"You," Henri said. "You speak English best, have the medical knowledge from helping Maman. Pierre and I will maintain the farm, keep routines normal."

She wanted to protest the designation but couldn't. It made sense, which didn't make it easier. Caring for an enemy pilot—because that's what the Reich would call him—meant accepting responsibility for his life and their deaths if discovered.

That evening, as purple shadows claimed the valley, she climbed again to check on their patient. James was conscious, fever giving his eyes an otherworldly brightness.

"Still here," he said. "Thought I might have dreamed you. Angels speaking French, offering salvation."

"No angels. Just farmers with more conscience than sense." She checked his temperature—too high, but not critically so. "Tell me about yourself. If we're risking our lives, I should know for whom."

So he talked, voice wandering through fever. Yorkshire childhood, university interrupted by war, training that turned farmers' sons into bomber pilots. His crew, young men who'd become brothers in the air, now scattered across French soil. The girl he'd left behind—Catherine, who wrote weekly letters he'd never now receive.

"What about you?" he asked when exhaustion forced a pause. "What's your story, besides saving fools who fall from the sky?"

"No story. Just lavender and survival." But she found herself talking too—about her mother's death, the farm's slow strangulation under occupation, Pierre's dangerous enthusiasm for resistance heroics. Things she hadn't spoken aloud, given voice by darkness and the strange intimacy of shared danger.

"Your English is excellent," he observed. "Unusual for a farmer's daughter."

"My mother was a teacher before marriage. She believed education was a form of resistance." Marguerite adjusted his blanket unnecessarily. "Fat lot of good it's done us."

"It's kept me alive. That seems fairly good."

"For now." She prepared to leave, then paused. "The Germans mentioned eight bodies recovered. Who else might have survived?"

Pain flickered across his features. "Tommy Morrison, our tail gunner. We bailed out together, but I lost him in the dark. He could be anywhere."

"Or he could be dead. The Germans are efficient about such things."

"Not efficient enough to find me."

"Yet." She left the word hanging, a reminder that survival was process, not achievement.

The next morning brought no patrols, no searches—just the careful routine of harvest and healing. Marguerite found herself looking forward to their conversations, James's perspective a window into a world beyond occupation. Pierre proved surprisingly capable at deception, his youthful enthusiasm masking genuine competence. Henri watched them all with the weight of final responsibility, counting days like a man defusing a bomb.

By the third day, James's fever had broken. She found him attempting to sit up, color better though pain still etched lines around his eyes.

"Feeling heroic?" she asked, helping him settle against the wall.

"Feeling foolish. And grateful. And probably developing Stockholm syndrome for my captors."

"We're not your captors. Captors would have turned you over for the reward." She unwrapped his bandages, pleased to see healing beginning. "We're just idiots with a barn."

"Beautiful idiots with excellent medical skills." He caught her hand as she worked. "Marguerite—I need you to know. If they catch me, I'll say I forced you. Threatened your family. Whatever keeps you safe."

"Lies won't save us if they find you here. Better to focus on healing." But his touch was warm, his concern genuine, and she found herself not pulling away. "Tell me about Yorkshire. Paint me a picture of somewhere without occupation."

So he did, voice stronger now, describing green dales and stone walls, sheep dotting hillsides like clouds fallen to earth. A world that seemed impossibly distant from hidden spaces and calculated risks. She listened while redressing his wounds, letting his words build a sanctuary neither of them could reach.

"Will you go back?" she asked. "When you heal, will you fly again?"

"If they'll let me. Though after this, might prefer ground duties." He managed a crooked smile. "Farming, perhaps. I've heard French lavender is lovely."

"It is. When it's not hiding fugitives." She finished with the bandages. "Rest now. In four days, you'll need to be strong enough to travel."

"Marguerite." He called her back as she moved to leave. "Why are you really doing this? Your family's already lost so much."

She considered the question, standing at the ladder's top. "Because the mathematics of loss don't improve by adding cowardice. Because my mother apparently believed in impossible things. Because..." She paused, finding truth in the shadows. "Because in this war, saving one life feels like defying all the death. Even temporarily."

"Temporarily is all any of us have." His eyes held hers across the dim space. "Make it count."

She descended without answering, but his words followed her into the night. Make it count. As if they had any choice now but to see this through, wherever it led.

One week. Seven days to heal a stranger and preserve their own lives. The arithmetic was simple, brutal, and offered no guarantee of survival. But for the first time since her mother's death, Marguerite felt the dangerous stirring of something beyond mere endurance.

Hope, perhaps. Or the beginning of love.

2

THE HIDDEN PILOT

AUGUST 1942 (THE WEEK FOLLOWING THE CRASH)

The hidden loft in the goat shed became James Crawford's world—a space barely six feet by eight, built by Marguerite's grandfather during the last war when suspicious farmers planned for desperate times. Marguerite had moved him there the night after his arrival, the cramped quarters offering better concealment than the open floor below. Dust motes danced in slivers of light that penetrated between weathered boards, and the scent of old hay mixed with the sharper smell of infection.

Each morning before dawn, she climbed the ladder with water and clean bandages, establishing a routine that felt both mundane and impossibly dangerous. Check his temperature, clean his wounds, assess the spreading infection that seemed to mock her efforts. Each evening, she returned with food and whatever medical supplies they could spare, stealing these moments of intimacy while the world raged beyond their sanctuary.

By the third day, the infection had worsened dramatically. Red streaks spread from the gash along his ribs like poisonous vines, and his skin burned with fever that no amount of cool water could break.

She unwrapped bandages that came away stained yellow-green, the smell making her stomach clench.

"You need a proper doctor," she whispered, keeping her voice low despite their isolation. In this hidden space, everything became whispers, every sound potentially treacherous.

"Can't risk it," James replied through gritted teeth, his accent thickened by pain. The fever had broken his usual politeness, stripping away everything but survival. "Besides, you're doing brilliantly."

"I'm a lavender farmer, not a nurse." She cleaned the wound with boiled water and precious wine, trying not to show her terror at the crimson streaks creeping toward his heart. Blood poisoning. Without proper medicine, he would die within days, and all their risks would be for nothing.

But she applied lavender honey to the wound anyway—an old remedy her grandmother had sworn by. The Dubois family had kept bees for generations, and their honey was prized throughout the valley for its healing properties. If anything could fight infection naturally, it would be this liquid gold that tasted of summer and hope.

He studied her as she worked, those impossibly blue eyes tracking every movement. She'd grown accustomed to his gaze over these few days, but not immune to it. There was something unsettling about being watched so intently, as if he were memorizing her face for future sketching.

"Tell me about before," he said suddenly, voice barely above a breath. "Before the war. What was life like here?"

She paused in her bandaging, startled by the request. "Why?"

"Because I need to imagine it. This place whole, untouched by Wehrmacht boots and Gestapo threats. Help me see what we're fighting to restore."

So she talked while she worked, painting word pictures of harvest festivals and market days, of her mother teaching in the village school and her father debating politics at the café. She described the annual lavender queen competition—which she'd won at eighteen, much to her embarrassment—and the Christmas markets that filled the square with light and laughter.

"There was a boy," she found herself saying, surprised by her own honesty. "Michel Rousseau. We were... we planned to marry after his military service. He was killed in Tunisia, early in the war. Twenty-two years old, and he'd never even seen the desert before they sent him there to die for France."

"I'm sorry." James's voice held genuine pain. "First love?"

"Only love." The admission came easier in the dimness. "I thought I'd have time for others, but then the war came, and..." She shrugged. "You don't replace someone like Michel. You just learn to carry the empty space."

"It sounds like paradise," James said when she finished describing the life they'd lost. "All of it. Even the heartbreak sounds clean compared to this."

"It was just life. We didn't know to treasure it until it was gone." She secured the last bandage, fingers lingering over the task. "What about you? What was your paradise?"

He closed his eyes, a smile playing at his lips despite the pain. "Yorkshire. Rolling green that stretches to forever. Sunday roasts at my mum's table, the whole family gathered round. Cricket matches that lasted all afternoon." His voice softened. "Catherine and I would walk the dales, planning our wedding, our future. She had the loveliest laugh —like silver bells on Christmas morning."

"Was?" Marguerite caught the past tense, though something in her chest tightened at hearing another woman's name spoken with such tenderness.

"The Coventry bombing. November last year." Pain flickered across his features, deeper than any physical wound. "She was visiting her sister, helping with the new baby. The house took a direct hit. They found..." He stopped, swallowing hard. "They found pieces. Enough to bury, barely."

"Oh, James." The words were inadequate, but she touched his hand anyway, offering what comfort she could. "I'm so sorry."

"We were to be married this Christmas. Had it all planned—church ceremony, reception at her father's farm, honeymoon in Scotland." His thumb traced circles on her palm. "Funny how you can plan a whole future that simply... ends. One night of German bombers, and twenty-three years of her life becomes memory."

They sat in silence, two people who'd learned too young that love was fragile, that war consumed everything tender and bright. The goat shed felt smaller somehow, their shared grief creating an intimacy more profound than physical closeness.

"The infection's getting worse," she said finally, professional concern overriding personal pain. "I can see the poison spreading. Without proper medicine..."

"I know." He squeezed her hand. "If it comes to that, promise me you'll let me go quietly. Don't risk yourselves trying to save a corpse."

"Don't be dramatic." But fear coursed through her. She couldn't watch another person she cared about die—and when had she started caring about this stranger who'd fallen from the sky? "I'm going to Valensole tomorrow. Dr. Bernard is discreet. He's helped before."

"Absolutely not." James struggled to sit up, pain making him gasp. "The risk—"

"The risk of you dying is greater than the risk of seeking help." She pressed him back down gently but firmly. "Trust me. I'll be careful."

She left before he could protest further, climbing down into the evening air that felt thin and cold after the closeness of the loft. Outside, Henri waited with Pierre, both their faces grim.

"How is he?" Henri asked.

"Dying." The word came out harsher than intended. "I need to go to Dr. Bernard tomorrow. Get proper medicine."

"Absolutely not," Henri echoed James's words. "Too dangerous."

"Everything's dangerous now, Papa. Hiding him is dangerous. Letting him die is dangerous. At least this way, he has a chance."

Pierre stepped forward, young face set with determination. "I'll go. They won't suspect a boy on errands for his family."

"No." Both Marguerite and Henri spoke simultaneously.

"I'm going," Marguerite said firmly. "I know what medicines to ask for, and I have a cover story. Female troubles requiring discretion— even Germans don't question too deeply about women's ailments."

Henri's face was stone, but he nodded slowly. "Take the bicycle. Be back before noon. And if anything feels wrong—anything at all—you turn around immediately."

The ride to Valensole the next morning felt endless, every German vehicle making her heart race. The medicine bag beneath her bread and vegetables seemed to radiate guilt, though she knew it contained nothing yet but hope. Her cover story rehearsed itself in her mind: monthly issues, need for discretion, embarrassment about personal matters.

Dr. Bernard's house sat on a quiet side street, its shuttered windows revealing nothing. His housekeeper, ancient Madame Reynard, answered the door with suspicious eyes that had seen too much during two wars.

"I need to see the doctor," Marguerite said, letting rural awkwardness creep into her voice. "It's urgent. Rather... personal."

"He's with a patient."

"I'll wait."

The waiting room smelled of carbolic and old fear. Marguerite counted heartbeats, imagined James growing weaker with each passing moment, wondered if this desperate gamble would save him or doom them all. Finally, the doctor emerged—white-haired, kind-eyed, carrying the weight of too many secrets.

"Mademoiselle Dubois. What brings you here?"

She glanced meaningfully at Madame Reynard. "Female troubles, Doctor. Rather urgent and... private."

He understood immediately, as she'd hoped he would. The Resistance had many friends among the medical community. "Of course. Come to my office."

Once the door closed, she spoke quickly, quietly. "I need antibiotics. Sulfa powder, penicillin if you have it. Morphine for pain."

His eyes sharpened. "That's quite a shopping list for female troubles."

"Please. I can't explain fully, but someone will die without help. Someone who's fighting the right fight."

"Allied?" At her nod, he moved to his medicine cabinet with practiced efficiency. "Pilot?"

"Does it matter?"

"Only for dosages." He selected several bottles, movements quick and sure. "Sulfa powder for wounds—apply directly twice daily. Morphine for pain, but careful with the dose. Too much kills as surely as too little helps. And this—" He produced a precious vial. "Penicillin. Worth its weight in gold and harder to find than diamonds."

"How did you—"

"Better you don't know." He packed everything into her market bag, hidden beneath vegetables and wrapped bread. "Follow the instructions exactly. And Mademoiselle? Don't come back here. If there are complications, send your brother with a message about visiting his 'sick grandmother' in Aix. I'll understand."

"Thank you. I can pay—"

"Keep your money. Consider it investment in the future we're all fighting for." His smile was sad. "I took an oath to do no harm. These days, that includes helping those who fight the harm-doers."

The ride home was terrifying, every checkpoint a potential disaster. But her papers were in order, her story believable, and sometimes courage was its own camouflage. She found Pierre anxiously watching the road, relief flooding his young face when she appeared.

"He's worse," Pierre reported immediately. "Calling out names, burning with fever. I've been bathing his face, but..."

They climbed to the loft together, Pierre proving surprisingly capable as she administered the precious medicines. The sulfa powder went directly into the wounds, the morphine carefully measured to ease pain without stopping his breathing. The penicillin was the real miracle—one injection now, others to follow if he survived.

James barely recognized her, lost in fever dreams that had him calling for Catherine, apologizing to shadows, reliving the crash over and over. She and Pierre took turns through the day, bathing his burning skin, forcing water between his lips, watching for signs that the medicine was working.

As evening approached, the fever finally broke. James opened his eyes, confused but lucid, focusing on Marguerite with effort.

"You came back," he said, voice raspy but real. "Thought I might have dreamed you."

"I'm persistently real." She helped him sip water, relief making her hands shake. "How do you feel?"

"Like I've been trampled by a herd of Yorkshire sheep. But alive."

His hand found hers, squeezing weakly. "The medicine—you took terrible risks."

"You were dying. The risk was necessary."

He studied her face in the lamplight, something shifting in his expression. "I remember calling for Catherine. Did I... did I say anything else?"

"Fever talk. Nothing important." But color rose in her cheeks, remembering his delirious murmurs of gratitude, his half-conscious attempts to touch her face.

"Marguerite." Her name in his accent did something to her insides, made the small space feel smaller. "I need to tell you something. About Catherine, about this—" He gestured between them. "I loved her. Will always love her memory. But she's gone, and I'm here, and what I'm feeling for you..."

"Don't." She pressed a finger to his lips, stopping the words that would change everything. "You're grateful. It's natural to—"

"It's not gratitude." He caught her hand, holding it against his mouth. "It's not fever or delirium or the romance of being rescued. It's you, Marguerite. Your courage, your kindness, the way you argue with me even when I'm half-dead. The way you've become the center of my world in just one week."

"It's only been a week," she whispered, but her protest was weak.

"In wartime, a week can be a lifetime. I know it's too soon, too complicated, too everything. But I love you, Marguerite Dubois. I know it's impossible, but—"

She stopped his words with her lips, pouring a week's worth of fear and hope and growing feelings into the kiss. It felt gentle as breathing, inevitable as sunrise—as if they'd been moving toward this moment since that first morning when she'd found him bleeding in their shed.

When they broke apart, both were breathless. James rested his forehead against hers, eyes closed.

"That was either the best idea or the worst idea in the history of terrible wartime decisions," he murmured.

"Probably both." She touched his face, amazed by the softness of his skin where the fever had broken. "This can't end well, you know. You'll have to leave. I have to stay. The war—"

"The war won't last forever."

"Won't it?" She pulled back slightly, though not far. "Even when the fighting stops, you'll go back to Yorkshire. I'll stay here with Papa and Pierre. Different worlds, different lives."

"Then we'll have whatever time we can steal before that happens." His thumb traced her cheekbone. "However many days or weeks until I'm strong enough to leave. That's more than many people get in wartime."

"It's not enough."

"No. But it's what we have." He drew her close again. "Let me love you while I can, Marguerite. Let us have this much, at least."

The plea in his voice undid her last defenses. She nodded, sealing their fate with a kiss that tasted of honey and desperate hope.

Their stolen time began that night. In the cramped sanctuary of the loft, they talked in whispers about everything and nothing—his childhood in the Yorkshire dales, her dreams of seeing Paris, the books they'd read, the futures they'd planned before war consumed everything. They shared stories and silence, touches that comforted and inflamed, the dangerous intimacy of two people falling in love in impossible circumstances.

Pierre proved himself worthy of trust, bringing meals and standing watch with new maturity. He asked no questions about the soft voices and occasional laughter from the loft, understanding somehow that his sister needed this brightness in the darkness surrounding them all.

Four days later, Pierre burst into the house during their morning meal, face flushed with exertion and alarm.

"Germans coming," he announced breathlessly. "Three vehicles from the village. More soldiers than usual—looks like a thorough search this time."

Henri was already moving, his limp more pronounced with urgency. "How much time?"

"Maybe ten minutes. They're stopping at farms along the way, but moving systematically." Pierre looked toward the goat shed. "What about—?"

"The loft space. Now." Henri grabbed his hunting rifle, though they all knew it was more symbol than protection against German efficiency. "This isn't routine. They're looking for something specific."

They moved with practiced urgency, James struggling to the hidden compartment despite obvious pain. Marguerite passed him water and medical supplies through the narrow opening before Pierre sealed the concealment with stacked hay bales.

"Remember," she whispered through the gap, "complete silence no matter what you hear."

The vehicles arrived precisely when expected—two trucks and a staff car, disgorging more soldiers than previous searches had brought. Sergeant Mueller emerged from the lead truck, but his usual bored efficiency had been replaced by sharp focus.

"Herr Dubois," Mueller called, approaching with formal military bearing. "We're conducting an intensive security sweep of this region. Recent intelligence suggests increased resistance activity."

"We've seen nothing unusual, Sergeant," Henri replied with careful deference. "Our work keeps us close to home."

"Perhaps. But intelligence sources indicate this area may be harboring enemies of the Reich." Mueller's pale eyes studied the farm with professional assessment. "We'll need to conduct a more thorough examination than previous visits."

The search proceeded with methodical German thoroughness. Soldiers spread through every building, every storage space, probing with the kind of systematic attention that had missed nothing in previous inspections. Marguerite stood with her family, outwardly calm while her heart hammered against her ribs.

When they reached the goat shed, she forced herself to look bored rather than terrified. The soldiers climbed to the loft, testing floorboards, examining every shadow. One paused directly above James's hiding place, flashlight beam playing across the concealing hay bales.

"Anything?" Mueller called from below.

"Empty storage. Hasn't been used in months." The soldier's boots shifted, weight pressing down inches from where James lay hidden. "Just dust and old straw."

Twenty endless minutes later, the search concluded. They'd found evidence of minor black market activity—some hidden oil, preserved vegetables—enough to justify suspicion but not enough to warrant arrests.

"Contraband goods," Mueller noted with satisfaction, examining their small cache. "Your father's arrest was clearly justified. Perhaps his family has learned the penalties for dishonesty?"

"We keep only what we need to survive," Marguerite replied carefully. "With Papa gone, we must be more careful about provisions."

"Indeed. Survival requires... adaptation." His gaze lingered on her face, noting the changes that weeks of stress had carved there. "We'll be conducting more frequent inspections in this area. I trust your family will remain cooperative?"

"Always, Sergeant. We want only to work our land in peace."

"Peace comes through obedience." He gestured to his men, who began withdrawing with professional efficiency. "Remember that compliance protects families. Resistance destroys them."

The convoy departed in clouds of dust and diesel fumes, leaving the farm violated but intact. They waited until engine sounds faded completely before moving to release James from his cramped concealment.

They found him unconscious, pain and stress having pushed him past endurance. His wounds had reopened from the strain of remaining motionless, blood seeping through bandages. But he was alive, undiscovered, and that had to be enough.

"That was too close," Henri said grimly as they helped James down from the loft. "They're not searching randomly anymore. Something has focused their attention on this area."

"The increased resistance activity Mueller mentioned," Pierre suggested. "More sabotage means more searches."

"Or someone's been talking." Marguerite cleaned James's reopened wounds with hands that wanted to shake. "Either way, you can't stay much longer. Each search brings them closer to finding you."

"I know." James struggled to sit up, accepting the bitter truth. "How long before the Resistance can move me?"

"Soon," she hoped, though she had no way of knowing. "Marie will have heard about today's search. She'll accelerate whatever plans exist."

That evening brought no BBC messages, no coded communications offering hope or timeline. They sat in tense silence, each lost in private fears about discovery, separation, and the impossible choices war demanded.

"The suspicions are definitely growing," Henri observed quietly. "Today felt different—more focused, more threatening. We may not have much time left."

"Then we make the most of what we have," Marguerite said, finding strength in necessity. "Whatever comes next, we face it together."

The German patrol had searched but not conquered, suspected but not discovered. James remained hidden, their secrets intact, their love preserved for however much time remained. It was a victory measured in hours rather than days, but in wartime, such victories were worth claiming.

Tomorrow would bring fresh dangers, new tests of courage and deception. But tonight, they were still whole, still united, still defiant against the forces trying to tear them apart.

The search had confirmed their worst fears—German suspicions were indeed growing, attention focusing on their small corner of occupied France. But it had also proven their defenses could hold, that love and determination could triumph over systematic oppression.

For now, it was enough. It had to be.

As evening approached, Marguerite climbed to the loft one more time to check on James. She found him attempting to exercise his good arm, moving carefully to protect healing wounds. The fever had broken completely, leaving him weak but clear-headed.

"You're recovering well," she observed, settling beside him in the cramped space that had become their sanctuary.

"Thanks to your care." He caught her hand, blue eyes holding depths that made her breath catch. "Marguerite, I need you to know something. These days with you—they've meant more than survival. You've given me hope when I'd lost it completely."

The intimacy of the moment, the knowledge that their time was running short, created a tension that seemed to fill the small space. Outside, the normal sounds of evening—Henri securing the barn, Pierre checking the chickens—felt distant, belonging to another world.

"I should go," she whispered, though she made no move to leave. "Let you rest."

"Stay," he said quietly. "Please. I know it's impossible, I know the dangers, but these might be our last nights together. When the Resistance comes..."

She silenced him with a kiss, pouring weeks of careful restraint into the contact. When they broke apart, both were breathing hard, the air between them charged with possibility and desperate need.

"Are you certain?" he whispered, hands trembling as they traced her face.

"I'm certain of nothing except this moment," she replied, drawing him closer. "Except you. Except us."

What followed was inevitable as sunrise, tender as prayer. In the lavender-scented darkness of their hidden sanctuary, they became lovers with desperate urgency, two souls clinging to beauty amid the chaos threatening to consume them. Every touch was discovery and farewell, every whispered endearment a defiance against the forces trying to tear them apart.

Afterward, they lay entwined on the narrow pallet, Marguerite's head on James's chest as he played with her unbound hair. The world had narrowed to this—heartbeats synchronized, breathing shared, love blooming in the most impossible soil.

"I love you," he said simply, words carrying the weight of absolute truth. "Whatever happens, whatever comes next, I need you to know that."

"I love you too." The admission came easily, naturally, as if her heart had been waiting her entire life to speak those words. "Always, James. Whatever happens."

They dozed fitfully, reluctant to surrender the intimacy that made them whole. Eventually, as the house settled around them, Marguerite slipped back to her own room, carrying with her the precious knowledge that some connections transcended circumstance, that love could exist even in war's shadow.

The next morning brought a new awareness between them—glances that lingered, touches that spoke of shared secrets, the knowledge that whatever came next, they had claimed something beautiful from the darkness.

That evening, after James had fallen into a fitful, fever-aided sleep, Marguerite descended from the loft, her heart heavy with their shared griefs and hopes. She found Henri and Pierre huddled by the hearth, the wireless crackling softly, its volume turned so low it was barely a whisper against the night's quiet. This was their ritual, a nightly act of defiance to connect with the world beyond their occupied valley.

"Anything?" she whispered, joining them.

Henri shook his head, his face illuminated by the radio's faint glow. "The usual. Troop movements near the coast, an address from de Gaulle..."

Suddenly, the announcer's voice shifted, becoming clipped and formal as he began the broadcast of seemingly nonsensical "personal messages." *'The baker has delivered the long loaf.' 'Jean's cat has climbed the tall tree.'* They listened intently, decoding hope from the mundane phrases. Then, a message came through that made the air in the small room go still.

"...The lavender angel tends her garden..."

The announcer repeated it once more before moving on. The three of them exchanged wide-eyed glances. It couldn't be a coincidence. Angel. Garden. Lavender. Someone knew. An unseen network of allies was aware of the English pilot bleeding in their goat shed, and of the young woman tending to him. The knowledge was both a comfort and a terror, a confirmation that they were not alone and a stark reminder of how far the news of their secret had already traveled.

"They know," Pierre breathed, a mixture of fear and romantic excitement in his eyes.

Henri simply switched off the wireless, the sudden silence heavier than the static had been. The risk had just grown immeasurably. It was this realization that solidified Marguerite's decision. Her practical care was no longer enough. James needed a miracle, and she would have to ride through enemy territory to find it.

"I need some air," she announced, escaping to the kitchen garden where her mother had once shelled peas and planned lessons.

The night was warm and still, perfumed with lavender and the last roses of summer. She sat on the familiar stone bench, trying to process the day's terror and the evening's revelation. James hidden in their shed, dependent on her care. Germans hunting with increasing desperation. The Resistance watching, waiting, sending coded hope through static-filled broadcasts.

"It's him, isn't it?" Pierre's voice made her jump. He stood silhouetted in the doorway, young face serious in the moonlight. "The message. They know about him."

She considered denying it, but Pierre deserved honesty. "Yes."

"How long before they come for him?"

"I don't know. Soon, probably. The network will want to move him before his presence endangers the whole area." The words tasted bitter. "Maybe days. Maybe a week."

"And then?"

"Then he goes to England. Back to his war." She touched the lavender growing wild beside the bench. "And we go back to ours."

Pierre sat beside her, brotherly warmth a comfort in the cooling night. "You love him."

It wasn't a question. "Is it that obvious?"

"To someone who knows you." His smile was sad. "Does he love you back?"

"He says he does." The memory of James's declaration, of their stolen kisses, brought both joy and pain. "But what does love mean in wartime? Everything's heightened, desperate. People cling to whatever light they find."

"Maybe that's when love means the most," Pierre said with unexpected wisdom. "When everything else is darkness."

They sat in comfortable silence, siblings united by shared secrets and impossible circumstances. Above them, stars wheeled indifferent to human suffering, and somewhere in England, people who'd never met them cared enough to send coded messages of hope.

"Do you think we'll survive this?" Pierre asked eventually.

"We've survived so far," she replied, the same answer she'd given weeks ago that felt like years.

"But will we survive it whole? Will there be anything left of who we were before?"

The question hung in the night air, heavy with implications. Would any of them emerge from this war unchanged? Would the gentle people they'd been before survive the brutal choices they were forced to make?

"I don't know," she admitted. "But we'll be who we need to be to protect each other. That's all anyone can do."

When she returned to check on James later that night, she found him sitting up properly for the first time, color almost normal in the lamplight. The medicines had worked their miracle, pulling him back from death's edge.

"You look almost human again," she observed, settling beside him in their small sanctuary.

"Feel it too. Your Dr. Bernard works miracles." He caught her hand, studying her face. "Something's troubling you. More than the usual impossible situation, I mean."

She told him about the radio message, watching recognition dawn in his eyes. "They know where you are. Help is coming."

"Soon?"

"I don't know. Soon enough." She pressed his palm to her cheek, memorizing the feeling. "I should be happy. You'll be safe, back with your own people."

"But?"

"But I'm not ready to lose you." The admission came easier in darkness. "I know it's selfish. I know you need to go. But these stolen moments we've had... they've meant everything."

"To me too." He drew her close, letting her rest against his shoulder. "More than everything. You've given me back my life, my hope, my heart. Whatever happens next, I'll carry you with me always."

"Promise me something," she whispered against his throat.

"Anything."

"When you get back to England, when this becomes just a story you tell... remember that it was real. That we were real, even if only for these few weeks."

"How could I forget?" His arms tightened around her. "You're carved into my soul now, Marguerite Dubois. War might separate us, but it can't erase this."

They held each other in the lavender-scented darkness, two people in love with impossible circumstances and borrowed time. Outside their sanctuary, the war raged on, bringing new dangers with each dawn. But for these stolen hours, they had found something pure and precious—a love that bloomed despite everything trying to kill it.

Tomorrow would bring fresh terrors, new tests of courage and commitment. But tonight, in their hidden space above the goat shed, they had each other. In wartime, it was more than most people got. In their hearts, it was everything.

The lavender angel tended her garden, and love grew in the darkest soil of all—the torn earth of a world at war.

❧ 3 ❧

NIGHT OF FIRE

AUGUST 1942 (THE FINAL DAY OF JAMES'S RECOVERY WEEK)

The SS arrived like death in tailored uniforms.

Marguerite watched from the kitchen window as three black vehicles swept into their courtyard with choreographed precision, raising dust that hung in the air like smoke from crematoriums. Six men emerged in perfect synchronization—not the bored efficiency of Wehrmacht soldiers conducting routine inspections, but something far more dangerous. These men moved with ideological certainty, each gesture suggesting this was neither their first raid nor their last.

"SS," Henri breathed, already moving toward the door. "Not Wehrmacht. SS."

Pierre stood frozen at the kitchen table, his face draining of color beneath his summer tan. "That's Hauptsturmführer Weiss. I know him."

"Know him how?" Marguerite demanded, her heart hammering against her ribs.

"From the village. He was asking questions about the Kellerman children last month. And he..." Pierre swallowed hard. "He was there when the Tessier family disappeared. Personally supervised their arrest."

The Kellerman children. The ones their mother had hidden, had saved. If Weiss was connecting those dots to their family...

"How much time?" Henri asked, his voice deadly calm.

"Minutes. Maybe less." Marguerite was already moving. "The root cellar. Behind the wine barrels."

She ran for the goat shed, finding James attempting to stand despite the pain etched across his features. A week of healing had strengthened him considerably, but his broken leg still couldn't bear full weight.

"I heard the engines," he said. "Different sound from regular patrols."

"SS. Much worse than regular army." She supported his weight as they moved toward the door. "Can you manage the cellar?"

"I'll bloody well manage anything to keep you safe."

They half-carried, half-dragged him across the yard, every second stretching like an eternity. The root cellar was cool and dark, smelling of earth and fermentation from Henri's carefully hoarded wine. Pierre appeared beside them, shoving heavy barrels aside with strength born of desperation, revealing the narrow space their father had built behind false boards during the last war.

"In," Marguerite ordered, helping James squeeze into the conceal-ment. "Don't move, don't breathe loudly, don't exist until we come for you."

"Marguerite—" His hand caught hers, grip fierce despite his weak-ness. "If they find me, you never saw me. I forced my way in, threat-ened your family. Promise me."

"They won't find you." She pressed her palm to his cheek, memo-rizing the feel of his skin. "But if the worst happens, save yourself. Don't die for us."

"Already too late for that," he said softly. "Be careful. Please."

Pierre shoved the barrels back into place as boots rang on cobble-stones above. They emerged from the cellar to find Henri facing the SS officer in their courtyard, the man studying their farm with calculating pale eyes.

Hauptsturmführer Weiss was younger than Marguerite had expected—perhaps thirty-five, with sharp features that might have been handsome without the uniform's sinister context. His French was perfect, devoid of any accent, which somehow made it more threatening than Mueller's struggling attempts.

"Herr Dubois," he said pleasantly, pulling out a silver cigarette case with practiced elegance. "I apologize for the intrusion. We're conducting an intensive investigation of farms that may have assisted enemies of the Reich."

"We assist no one, Hauptsturmführer," Henri replied with careful deference. "We barely manage to assist ourselves. As Sergeant Mueller can attest, we struggle to meet even our quotas."

"Yes, Mueller. Adequate soldier, poor judge of character." Weiss lit a cigarette with a gold lighter that caught the afternoon sun, the gesture oddly civilized. "Tell me, you have children, yes? A daughter and son?"

It wasn't a question. He already knew.

"Yes, Hauptsturmführer," Henri said carefully.

Weiss's pale eyes found Marguerite, studying her with uncomfortable intensity. "You must be the daughter. The one who speaks such excellent English."

The knowledge hit like ice water. How did he know about her languages?

"I speak some English," she admitted, keeping her voice level. "My mother was a teacher before the war. She believed education was important."

"Was. Yes, your mother. The late Amélie Dubois, schoolteacher at the école primaire." Weiss drew on his cigarette, smoke curling around his words. "Such a tragedy, her passing. Cancer, wasn't it? Particularly unfortunate—educated women are so... useful in times like these."

A trap within a trap. Every word calculated to probe for reactions, to test their knowledge and loyalties.

"Maman helped children learn to read," Marguerite said simply. "Nothing that would interest the Reich."

"Oh, but reading is very interesting to the Reich. We are great believers in education. Records. Documentation." His smile was razor-thin. "Your mother had access to student records, family information. Names and addresses of every child in the village."

"She taught French grammar and arithmetic," Pierre interjected, his young voice steady despite the danger. "Basic lessons for farming children."

"The boy speaks!" Weiss turned his attention to Pierre with predatory interest. "Seventeen years old, are you not? Prime age for the Service du travail obligatoire. Why haven't you reported for labor service in Germany?"

"Agricultural exemption," Henri answered quickly. "The farm requires—"

"I asked the boy." Weiss's voice remained pleasant, but steel showed beneath the courtesy. "Can he not speak for himself?"

Pierre straightened, meeting the officer's gaze with surprising courage. "I have proper exemption papers, Hauptsturmführer. Would you like to examine them?"

"Later, perhaps. First, let's discuss your mother's extracurricular activities." Weiss gestured to his men, who began spreading through the property with methodical efficiency. "You see, we've been tracking certain... irregularities. Jewish children who disappeared from official records. Families who vanished just before scheduled relocations."

The mathematics of terror: connect Amélie's access to student records with missing Jewish children, and their family became guilty by association. Marguerite kept her face carefully neutral while her mind raced through possibilities.

"I wouldn't know about such things," she said. "Maman protected us from the war's complications."

"Protected. Yes, mothers do that." Weiss dropped his cigarette, grinding it beneath his heel with unnecessary force. "Even when protection becomes collaboration with enemies of the state."

Before anyone could respond, a shout echoed from the direction of the goat shed. One of the SS soldiers emerged holding something that made Marguerite's stomach plummet—James's bloodied flight jacket, the one they'd stupidly kept meaning to burn.

"Hauptsturmführer," the soldier called. "Found this hidden behind feed sacks."

Weiss examined the garment with professional interest, noting the RAF insignia, the recent damage, the blood still dark on torn fabric. "Interesting. British manufacture. Recent damage. Blood relatively fresh." He looked up, pale eyes bright with satisfaction. "Care to explain?"

Henri stepped forward without hesitation. "We found it three days ago, caught on fence wire in the eastern field. Kept meaning to turn it in, but with harvest demands—"

"Please." Weiss held up a hand, his smile sharpening. "Let's not insult each other's intelligence. This jacket was worn recently, bled in recently. More importantly, it was hidden recently." He gestured to his men. "Expand the search. Every building, every cellar, every possible concealment. Someone has been playing host to an Allied airman."

Marguerite's heart hammered so violently she was certain it must be visible. Below their feet, James lay hidden in a space barely large enough for breathing, surrounded by SS boots that would kill him instantly if discovered. The mathematics had shifted catastrophically: no longer if they would be caught, but when.

"Hauptsturmführer!" Another voice interrupted from across the yard. A young SS soldier approached with urgent steps. "Radio message from headquarters. Resistance activity reported near Manosque. All units ordered to respond immediately."

Weiss's expression flickered with annoyance. "Now? In the middle of this?"

"General Koenig insists, sir. Full response required within the hour."

For a long moment, Weiss stood perfectly still, silver cigarette case turning in his fingers like worry beads. The air grew thick with unspoken threats as he calculated options, weighing the competing demands of duty and suspicion.

Finally, he smiled—an expression somehow worse than any scowl.

"Very well. We'll continue this conversation later." He stepped close to Henri, voice dropping to an intimate whisper. "I know you're hiding something, Herr Dubois. Or someone. When I return—and I will return very soon—I'll find what you've concealed. And then we'll discuss the penalties for harboring enemies of the Reich."

The threat hung in the air like poison gas as the SS withdrew with the same choreographed precision they'd arrived with. Black vehicles rolled away, leaving behind trampled garden beds and the lingering scent of expensive tobacco.

The family stood frozen until engine sounds faded completely into afternoon silence.

"The cellar," Marguerite whispered, already running.

They pulled James from concealment to find him conscious but shaking, stress and confinement having pushed him toward shock. His hands trembled as she helped him stand, the week of healing undone by terror and cramped positioning.

"They're gone?" he asked, voice barely audible.

"For now. But they'll be back." Henri's face was granite. "Tonight, tomorrow—Weiss isn't finished with us."

"Then I leave now," James said immediately. "Before I bring more danger—"

"You can barely stand," Marguerite protested, steadying him as he swayed. "Look at you—"

"Better I die trying to escape than watch them execute your family." His blue eyes found hers, desperate with protective instinct. "I won't be the cause of your deaths."

"No one's dying today," a new voice said from the doorway.

They spun to find Marie Beaumont standing in the entrance, egg basket over her arm as if this were merely a social call. Their neighbor looked exactly as always—weathered face, practical dress, expression suggesting nothing more complex than poultry concerns.

"Marie," Henri said carefully, moving to block her view of James. "We weren't expecting—"

"No, but you were hoping. Wondering who might help with your current difficulty." She entered uninvited, setting down her basket and moving toward James with movements that suddenly seemed too practiced for a simple farmer's wife. "RAF, I assume? You've done well keeping him alive this long."

The casual acknowledgment struck them speechless. Marie knelt beside James, checking his pulse with professional efficiency, lifting an eyelid to examine his pupils.

"How did you—" Marguerite began.

"Know? Child, half the valley heard something crash in the hills. The question is who's foolish enough to have kept what fell." She pulled a small bottle from her egg basket—morphine, medical grade. "Shock and stress injuries. This will help."

She administered the injection with disturbing expertise, hands steady as any doctor's. The morphine worked quickly, easing the tremors from James's frame as the Dubois family recalibrated their understanding of their egg-selling neighbor.

"Marie," Henri said slowly. "What exactly are you?"

"Someone who knew your wife very well." Marie's weathered hands were gentle as she examined James's healing wounds. "Someone who shared certain... interests with Amélie regarding the welfare of displaced persons."

"The Kellerman children," Pierre breathed. "You helped Maman hide them."

"Among others. Your mother was remarkable—used her position at the school to identify families at risk, coordinate safe passage." Marie's voice carried deep affection. "She never told you, did she? Wanted to protect you from the knowledge, the danger."

"But you knew," Marguerite said, pieces clicking into place. "All this time, you knew what she was doing."

"I was her primary contact with the network. Have been for three years." Marie stood, brushing her hands clean. "Which brings us to the current crisis. This pilot needs to disappear tonight, before Weiss returns. I can arrange transport."

"Where?" Henri asked.

"Abandoned shepherd's hut in the hills, as a temporary measure. From there, the escape line through Spain." Marie's gaze found Marguerite. "But there are conditions."

"What conditions?"

"The network requires assets in place. Intelligence sources. With your father now under suspicion, we need someone clean, someone positioned to gather information." Marie's expression grew serious.

"There's a position at the mairie—clerk in the administrative office. Access to German correspondence, travel permits, operation schedules. I've already arranged the interview."

"You want me to spy."

"I want you to survive. Active participation offers protection you won't find hiding on this farm." Marie pulled fresh supplies from her seemingly innocent basket—bandages, medicines, travel rations. "Make your choice quickly. We have perhaps two hours before full darkness."

Marguerite looked at James, seeing her own conflict reflected in his eyes. Stay together and risk everyone, or separate and serve the larger cause. The mathematics of resistance offered no clean solutions.

"If I take this position," she said slowly, "what happens to Papa and Pierre?"

"They maintain the farm, play the part of simple farmers intimidated by SS attention. Rural stupidity as camouflage." Marie began packing supplies into a travel bag. "Your absence for 'work' explains any changes in behavior."

"And James?"

"Moves tonight to the shepherd's hut. From there, depending on his recovery, either immediate extraction or a longer stay until he's fit for mountain travel."

"How long?" James asked, the morphine allowing him to focus despite obvious pain.

"Days. Weeks. However long it takes." Marie's tone brooked no argument. "The escape routes have their own schedules, their own priorities. You wait your turn."

"I won't leave her exposed while I hide in the hills," James said firmly. "If she's taking this position, risking herself—"

"You'll do whatever serves the mission," Marie interrupted. "Both of you. Personal feelings are luxuries we can't afford."

The words stung because they were true. Marguerite pressed her palms to her eyes, trying to think past emotion to logic. Taking the position would give her purpose, access, the chance to help others like James. Staying would doom them all when Weiss returned.

"I'll do it," she said quietly. "Take the position."

"Marguerite—" James reached for her hand.

"It's the right choice." She squeezed his fingers, memorizing their warmth. "The only choice that saves everyone."

"The interview is tomorrow morning," Marie said with satisfaction. "Tonight, we move the pilot. Henri, you'll help with transport. Pierre, you maintain watch here."

"What about the SS? When they return?"

"They'll find a farm family properly intimidated by official attention. Marguerite away at her new position, James never existed." Marie shouldered the travel bag. "The shepherd's hut has been used before— well-supplied, defensible. He'll be safe until extraction."

The next hours blurred with preparation. Marie produced civilian clothes for James, papers identifying him as a injured farmworker from Normandy. His broken leg was re-splinted for travel, wounds redressed with clean bandages. The morphine helped, but moving still brought obvious pain.

"This isn't how I wanted to leave," he said as they prepared for his departure. Twilight was falling, providing cover for movement. "Not like this, with you going into danger."

"Nothing about this situation is how anyone wanted." Marguerite adjusted his sling, fingers lingering on the task. "But it's what we have."

"When this war ends—" he began.

"Don't." She pressed a finger to his lips. "No promises. No plans. Just... remember that this was real."

"How could I forget?" He caught her hand, pressing it to his cheek. "You saved my life, Marguerite Dubois. In every way that matters."

"You saved mine too. Gave me purpose beyond simple survival."

Henri appeared in the doorway, rifle in hand and pack on his back. "Time to go. Marie's waiting with the cart."

James struggled to his feet, accepting Henri's support with obvious reluctance. At the door, he turned back to Marguerite, blue eyes memorizing her face in the lamp light.

"The lavender will bloom again," he said softly. "After all this madness ends, it will bloom again."

"I'll be waiting," she replied, though they both knew the impossibility of such certainty.

He nodded once, then followed Henri into the gathering darkness. Marguerite watched from the window as they disappeared into night, taking with them the stolen week of impossible love and leaving behind only memory and the weight of choices made.

Pierre joined her at the window, young face grave with new understanding. "Will we see him again?"

"I don't know." She touched the glass where his shadow had passed. "But we'll remember him. And maybe, if we're very fortunate and the war doesn't last forever, remembering will be enough."

"And if it's not?"

"Then we'll have loved truly once, in the darkest time. That's more than many people get."

Outside, the lavender fields stretched purple in moonlight, holding their ancient secrets. Tomorrow would bring new dangers, new deceptions, new choices between survival and conscience. But tonight, in the space between what was lost and what might still be saved, love had bloomed despite everything trying to kill it.

The night of fire had passed, leaving them changed but unbroken. Now came the harder test—living with the choices they'd made, serving causes larger than their hearts, finding courage for the long darkness still ahead.

In the hills, James settled into his temporary sanctuary, while Marguerite prepared for her new role in the deadly game of resistance. Separated but not severed, they carried each other's memory into an uncertain future.

The war would continue. Love would endure. And somewhere in the space between, hope would bloom again when lavender returned to the fields.

◈❧◈

❧ 4 ❧

THE ARREST

Henri Dubois believed in the power of routine. Even in the chaos of occupation, even with an SS officer's threats hanging over his family like a sword, he maintained his Thursday morning ritual—coffee at the Café des Platanes in Valensole's market square. Weak ersatz that barely resembled coffee, served in chipped cups by a proprietor who'd lost two sons to German labor conscription, but still coffee. Still routine. Still a small act of defiance against the forces trying to strip away everything familiar.

"Routine is sanity," he'd told Marguerite that morning, adjusting his hat with the same careful precision he'd used for twenty years. "When everything else is madness, routine reminds us who we were before the world went wrong."

She'd wanted to argue, to beg him to stay home where it was safer. But Henri Dubois was a stubborn man, hardened by one war and determined not to let another break his spirit. So she'd kissed his weathered cheek and watched him limp down the lane, Verdun's old wound making his gait distinctive even at distance.

Now, standing frozen in the market square with her shopping

39

basket clutched in white-knuckled hands, she watched that stubborn spirit finally meet its match.

"Henri Dubois!" The voice cut through market chatter like a blade through silk. "By order of the Reich, you are under arrest!"

The world telescoped, sounds becoming distant and hollow. Marguerite saw her father rise from his usual table outside the café, saw the coffee cup fall from nerveless fingers to shatter on cobblestones. Saw Hauptsturmführer Weiss emerge from the shadows where he'd been waiting—how long had he been waiting?—flanked by six SS soldiers whose black uniforms seemed to absorb the morning light.

"There must be some mistake," Henri said with dignity that broke her heart. "I'm a simple farmer—"

"Simple farmers don't harbor enemies of the Reich." Weiss gestured, and soldiers moved with practiced efficiency, snapping metal handcuffs around Henri's wrists. "Simple farmers don't conceal agricultural production from official requisitions. Simple farmers don't collaborate with terrorist networks."

The charges rolled out in Weiss's cultured French, each accusation finding its mark. Conspiracy against the Reich. Harboring enemies of the state. Economic sabotage. A mixture of truth and fabrication that would be impossible to deny or prove, depending on what the SS chose to believe.

Around the square, vendors and customers melted away like morning mist. Market stalls emptied, conversations died, the normal bustle of commerce replaced by the terrible silence that followed official violence. Only Marguerite remained frozen in place, basket handle cutting into her palm, watching her world collapse in broad daylight.

"Papa!" The cry tore from her throat before she could stop it.

Henri's eyes found hers across the square, wide with warning and desperate love. "Stay back," he mouthed, but she was already pushing through the ring of soldiers, maternal instinct overriding sense.

"There must be a mistake," she said to Weiss, hating the pleading in her voice but unable to stop it. "My father is loyal to the Reich. He's done nothing—"

"Your father," Weiss interrupted with silky malice, "has done many things. We have evidence of hidden stores, black market dealings, possible connection to the downed enemy pilot you've been harboring."

The accusation hit like a physical blow. For a moment, the square spun around her, black spots dancing at the edges of her vision. He knew. Somehow, despite their precautions, despite James being safely hidden in the shepherd's hut, Weiss knew.

"I don't know what you mean," she managed, surprised by the steadiness of her own voice.

"Don't you?" Weiss stepped closer, pale eyes studying her face like a scientist examining specimens. "Such an innocent expression. Almost believable." His smile was razor-thin. "Your father was less convincing during preliminary questioning."

"What questioning? When did you—"

"This morning, before dawn. While you slept peacefully in your bed, we had an illuminating conversation with Herr Dubois about his recent activities." Weiss pulled out his silver cigarette case, the gesture oddly civilized amid the brutality. "He was remarkably resistant to persuasion. Admirable loyalty, if misguided."

Marguerite looked at her father, seeing for the first time the bruising around his left eye, the careful way he held his ribs. They'd already hurt him, already begun the process of breaking him down piece by piece.

"Marguerite," Henri called out, his voice carrying layers of meaning only she could understand. "Go home. Take care of the farm." His eyes bored into hers, willing her to comprehend. "Take care of everything."

James. He was telling her to protect James, to ensure their hidden pilot stayed hidden no matter what happened to him. Even facing imprisonment and torture, Henri Dubois was thinking of others first.

"Listen to your father," Weiss advised with mock kindness. "Run along home, little farmer. Unless you'd prefer to join him? I'm sure we could find evidence of your crimes as well."

The threat was explicit, delivered with the casual cruelty of a man who held absolute power. Marguerite stepped back, every instinct screaming at her to fight, to throw herself at these black-uniformed monsters and claw at their faces until they released her father. But that would only confirm their suspicions, only give them excuse to arrest her too.

"Where are you taking him?" she asked, proud that her voice didn't shake.

"Marseille for proper interrogation. After that..." Weiss shrugged eloquently. "That depends on his cooperation. And yours."

They loaded Henri into the waiting truck with rough efficiency, treating him like cargo rather than human being. He sat straight-backed among other arrested men—she recognized Monsieur Delorme the baker, two farmers from neighboring valleys, all guilty of the universal crime of surviving under occupation.

"One week," Weiss said as the truck's engine coughed to life. "You have one week to prove your innocence, Mademoiselle Dubois. After that, family reunions may become... unavoidable."

The truck rumbled away in a cloud of diesel fumes, carrying her father toward an uncertain fate. Marguerite stood alone in the emptied square, basket still clutched in her hands, watching until the vehicle disappeared around the curve toward Marseille.

"Marguerite." A gentle hand touched her shoulder. She turned to find Sylvie Gérard, the young woman's pretty face streaked with tears. "I'm so sorry. If there's anything I can do—"

"Look after my purchases," Marguerite said mechanically, setting down the basket she'd forgotten she was holding. "I need to get home. Pierre doesn't know yet."

The bicycle ride back to the farm passed in a blur of grief and terror. Her father was gone, their protector removed, their secrets exposed to SS scrutiny. How long before Weiss connected all the pieces? How long before he found James despite their precautions?

She found Pierre in the lavender fields, cutting stems with the same methodical precision their father had taught them. His young face lit up at her early return, then crumbled as he registered her expression.

"What happened? You look like—"

"Papa's been arrested." The words came out flat, drained of emotion she couldn't afford to feel yet. "At the market. SS took him to Marseille for interrogation."

The cutting blade slipped from Pierre's hand, clattering among the purple stems. "No. That's not—he was just having coffee. His Thursday coffee. He always—"

"They knew about the hidden stores. About the black market trading." She gripped his shoulders as seventeen-year-old bravado dissolved into childish tears. "Listen to me. We have to be strong now. We have to think."

"Think about what? They have Papa! They'll torture him for information, send him to a camp, we'll never see him again—"

"Stop." She shook him gently but firmly. "Papa is tough. He survived Verdun, he can survive this. But right now we have to protect what he was protecting. Do you understand?"

Pierre's eyes widened with comprehension. "James. If they search the farm again, if they find him—"

"They will search. Count on it. Which means we need to move him immediately."

"But where? The shepherd's hut isn't safe if they're actively hunting him. And he's still not fully healed—"

Marguerite's mind raced through possibilities. They needed somewhere secure, somewhere the SS wouldn't think to look, somewhere that could provide James with medical care while the Resistance arranged his extraction.

"The monastery," she said suddenly. "Séguret. Brother Benedict mentioned they sometimes provide sanctuary for travelers in need."

"The Benedictines? But they're not supposed to get involved in politics—"

"Helping injured people isn't politics, it's Christian charity." At least, she hoped the monks would see it that way. "It's our only option. James can't stay in the hills alone, not with Weiss hunting him specifically."

They worked with desperate efficiency, gathering supplies and preparing for another dangerous journey. James would need to be moved in daylight—risky, but less suspicious than nighttime activity that might draw patrol attention. They'd take the farm cart, claim they were delivering produce to the monastery's kitchen as they'd done occasionally before the war.

The ride to the shepherd's hut felt endless, every sound making them jump. German patrols were everywhere now, search parties combing the hills for any sign of the missing pilot. But luck held—they reached the stone refuge without encountering soldiers.

James was awake when they arrived, attempting to exercise his healing leg with careful movements. He looked up at their entrance, smile dying at their expressions.

"What's happened?"

"My father's been arrested," Marguerite said without preamble. "SS took him this morning. They know about the hidden stores, suspect about you. We have to move you now."

"Christ." He struggled to his feet, accepting the news with grim resignation. "I'm sorry. This is because of me—"

"This is because of the war," she interrupted. "Because good people tried to help others and evil people won't tolerate it. But we're not finished yet."

She explained their plan as they prepared him for travel—the monastery at Séguret, the hope that Benedictine traditions of sanctuary would protect him until proper extraction could be arranged. James listened with the focused attention of a man calculating survival odds.

"The monks will hide me? A Protestant Englishman who's brought death to their doorstep?"

"They'll hide an injured human being who needs help," she said firmly. "Brother Benedict is a good man. He'll understand."

"And if he doesn't?"

"Then we find another option. But right now, this is what we have."

They loaded him into the cart beneath sacks of vegetables and lavender, creating the illusion of a routine delivery. James bore the discomfort stoically, though she could see pain in his tight-pressed lips when the cart jolted over rough ground.

The monastery of Séguret perched on a hillside overlooking the valley, its ancient stones weathered by centuries of mistral winds. Marguerite had visited occasionally with her mother, bringing produce to trade for the excellent cheese the brothers made. Now she prayed that Christian charity would extend to more than commerce.

Brother Benedict met them at the gate, his round face creased with concern. "Marguerite, my child. I heard about your father's arrest. Terrible business."

"News travels fast," she said carefully.

"Bad news always does. How can we help?" His kind eyes took in Pierre's pale face, the cart loaded with more supplies than a simple delivery would require. "Are you in need of sanctuary?"

The question was asked quietly, meaningfully. Brother Benedict might be a man of God, but he wasn't naive about the world's complexities.

"We have a friend," she said, meeting his gaze directly. "An injured traveler who needs safe shelter while arrangements are made for his journey home."

"What manner of traveler?"

"The kind who fell from the sky while fighting those who would destroy everything good in this world."

Brother Benedict was silent for a long moment, studying her face. Then he nodded slowly. "Bring him inside. Quietly."

They helped James from the cart, supporting his weight as they followed the monk through corridors that had sheltered refugees and pilgrims for eight hundred years. Brother Benedict led them to a small cell in the monastery's oldest section, simply furnished but clean and secure.

"He'll be safe here," the monk assured them as they settled James on the narrow bed. "The community has experience with... difficult guests. But you must understand—this can only be temporary. A few days, perhaps a week."

"Thank you," James said in careful French. "I know the danger you're accepting."

"Danger is everywhere these days," Brother Benedict replied pragmatically. "At least this danger serves God's purposes. Rest now. Brother Matthias will tend your wounds—he was a medic in the last war."

As they prepared to leave, Marguerite knelt beside James's bed for what might be their final private moment. His hand found hers, squeezing gently.

"This isn't how I wanted to say goodbye," he whispered.

"It's not goodbye. It's temporary separation while we both do what we must." She leaned down to kiss him softly. "Stay alive, James Crawford. When this war ends, I want to show you the lavender fields in bloom."

"I'll hold you to that promise."

"It's not a promise," she said, though her eyes said otherwise. "It's a threat."

The ride home was subdued, both siblings lost in their own thoughts. The farm felt empty without Henri's presence, abandoned despite their continued occupation. They went through the motions of evening chores, fed the remaining chickens, checked the lavender fields for signs of damage from the morning's search.

As darkness fell, Marguerite stood in the doorway looking out at the valley where her family had farmed for generations. Her father was in SS custody, facing torture and possible death. James was hidden in a monastery, dependent on monastic charity and Resistance connections she wasn't sure existed. The farm that had been their sanctuary was now a trap, watched and suspected.

But they were still alive. Still free. Still fighting in whatever small ways they could.

"What do we do now?" Pierre asked, joining her in the doorway.

"We survive," she said simply. "We maintain the farm, play the part of a grieving family intimidated by official attention. And we trust that Papa's strength will hold, that James will reach safety, that good people will continue choosing courage over comfort."

"That's a lot of trust."

"It's all we have." She put her arm around him, drawing comfort from his solid presence. "But it's enough. It has to be enough."

In the distance, church bells chimed the hour—a sound that had marked time in this valley since before France was a nation, before wars and occupation and the terrible mathematics of survival. The bells would ring long after the current madness ended, marking ordinary hours for ordinary people living ordinary lives.

Marguerite held onto that thought as darkness deepened around them. Somewhere, her father fought to protect his family's secrets. Somewhere, James began another chapter of his long journey home.

And here, in the space between what was lost and what might still be saved, hope endured despite everything trying to kill it.

Tomorrow would bring new challenges, new choices between survival and conscience. Tonight, she would mourn what was lost and prepare for what was coming. Because in the end, that's all anyone could do—endure until endurance became its own form of victory.

The war had taken her father, but it hadn't broken her spirit. Not yet. Not ever, if she had anything to say about it.

৩১৯৩

❧ 5 ❧

THE RESISTANCE CONTACT

AUGUST 1942 (THE NIGHT OF HENRI'S ARREST)

T he ancient olive grove stood twisted and silvered in moonlight, its gnarled trees planted by Roman hands and shaped by centuries of mistral winds. Each shadow seemed to hold secrets, each rustle of leaves whispered of clandestine meetings that had shaped the valley's hidden history. Marguerite arrived early, every nerve singing with tension, her father's arrest weighing on her heart like a stone.

She'd left Pierre at the farm—someone had to maintain the pretense of normalcy if Germans came calling. The bruise on her cheek throbbed with each heartbeat, Weiss's casual violence a reminder of how quickly their situation was deteriorating. In a few hours, she'd have to be at the mairie, playing the role of grateful suppliant seeking employment. But first, this meeting that might change everything.

Marie Beaumont emerged from the shadows like a ghost made flesh, her familiar face transformed in the silver light. Gone was the neighborly egg seller who'd chatted about chickens and weather. In her place stood someone harder, more purposeful—a lifetime of careful camouflage dropped in the safety of darkness.

"Marguerite." Marie's voice held depths that had never been there during daylight conversations. "I'm sorry about your father. Henri is a good man caught in impossible circumstances."

"Do you have news of him?" Marguerite searched the older woman's face for hope or despair.

"He's alive. In La Prison Saint-Pierre in Marseille. The conditions are... difficult, but he endures." Marie studied her carefully. "You're wondering how I know this."

"I'm wondering many things." Marguerite settled onto a fallen log, ancient wood smooth beneath her fingers. "Starting with who you really are."

"Someone who knew your mother very well. Someone who shared certain... interests with Amélie regarding the welfare of displaced persons." Marie's weathered hands folded in her lap, steady despite the gravity of their conversation. "She never told you about her other work, did she?"

"What other work?" But even as she asked, pieces were falling into place—her mother's careful questions about German officers seen in the village, her uncanny knowledge of troop movements, the way conversations stopped when Marguerite entered rooms.

"Your mother was one of our most valuable assets," Marie said quietly. "She used her position as a schoolteacher and her language skills to gather intelligence from unsuspecting German officers. They would chat at school functions, never suspecting the quiet teacher was memorizing every detail of their conversations."

The revelation hit like a physical blow. Marguerite thought of her gentle mother, always so proper, so careful about appearances. "Maman was a spy?"

"Your mother was a patriot who understood that small acts of resistance could bloom into larger victories." Marie's voice carried old affection mixed with professional respect. "She had a gift for languages, for remembering conversations exactly. German officers felt safe speaking around her—what threat could a provincial schoolteacher pose?"

"But the risk..." Marguerite struggled to reconcile this revelation with her memories. "If they'd discovered her—"

"They would have shot her, yes. Or worse." Marie's matter-of-fact tone made the words more chilling. "Your mother understood the dangers better than most. But she also understood that information was a weapon, and she wielded it expertly."

"She never said anything. Never even hinted..."

"Because she was protecting you. The best resistants are invisible, especially women. Your mother taught you the same skills—to observe without seeming to, to listen more than you speak, to remember everything while revealing nothing." Marie leaned forward. "She trained you for this life whether you realized it or not."

Marguerite thought of all the lessons disguised as maternal guidance—the importance of learning languages, of blending into any situation, of keeping family secrets. Training for a war her mother had seen coming long before the first German boot crossed the frontier.

"She's gone now," Marguerite said flatly. "Whatever she was, whoever she really was—it died with her."

"Did it?" Marie's smile held bitter knowledge. "You've been harboring a British pilot for over a week. You've managed to keep him hidden from multiple German searches. You've established medical care and safe houses with nothing but instinct and determination. Those aren't the actions of someone untrained in resistance work."

The words hung in the night air, heavy with implication. Marguerite felt the weight of inherited purpose, a legacy she'd never asked for but couldn't ignore.

"What do you want from me?" she asked quietly.

"What your mother would have wanted—for you to use your gifts in service of something larger than survival." Marie pulled a small packet from her coat. "Your pilot needs immediate extraction. We can arrange it, but the network requires something in return."

"What kind of something?"

"Information. Access. The kind of intelligence that comes from working inside German administration." Marie's eyes gleamed in the moonlight. "There's a position opening at the mairie—clerical work, serving refreshments, filing papers. Mindless tasks for a simple farm girl seeking to support her family after her father's unfortunate arrest."

The pieces clicked into place with terrifying precision. "You want me to spy from inside the German headquarters."

"I want you to be your mother's daughter. To honor her legacy while serving your country." Marie's voice gentled. "The position is already arranged—Captain Weiss will approve your employment tomorrow, though he believes it was his idea."

"How could you possibly—"

"Your mother built an extensive network over three years of careful work. Some of those connections remain active, waiting for the right moment to act." Marie studied Marguerite's face. "This is that moment. Your father's arrest provides perfect cover—a desperate daughter seeking work to survive. Who would suspect such a person of gathering intelligence?"

"And if I refuse?"

"Then your pilot will still receive help, because it's the right thing to do. But your assistance would be... limited." Marie paused meaning-fully. "As would any efforts to help your father."

The threat was subtle but clear. Marguerite looked up at the stars wheeling overhead, the same constellations that had witnessed her mother's secret meetings, her grandmother's whispered prayers, gener-ations of Dubois women making impossible choices.

"James leaves tomorrow night?"

"If his condition allows. We're sending a doctor to assess him this afternoon—someone who asks no uncomfortable questions." Marie's expression softened slightly. "You can say goodbye, if you're careful about timing and location."

The word 'goodbye' hit like a blade between her ribs. She'd known this moment would come, but knowing and accepting were different creatures entirely.

"I'll do it," she heard herself say. "Work at the mairie, gather what intelligence I can. But I have conditions."

Marie's eyebrows rose. "You're hardly in a position to negotiate."

"Pierre stays out of this completely. He's seventeen—he deserves a chance at something resembling normal life after this madness ends."

Marguerite's voice grew firm. "And I want regular updates on James's progress. Not operational details, just confirmation that he lives."

"The first is reasonable. The second is dangerous sentimentality."

"It's my price for cooperation."

Marie considered for a long moment, then nodded slowly. "Very well. Though I warn you—caring too much about individual outcomes can compromise judgment. Your mother learned to compartmentalize her emotions for the greater good."

"I'm not my mother."

"No," Marie agreed. "You're younger, less patient, more inclined toward action than observation. Which could be an asset or a fatal flaw, depending on how you channel it." She stood, brushing dust from her skirt. "Meet me here tomorrow night after your pilot's extraction. We'll discuss operational procedures and communication protocols."

"Wait." Marguerite rose as well. "You said the monastery at Séguret would shelter James until the network could move him. Is that still the plan?"

"Brother Benedict has agreed to provide sanctuary, yes. The Benedictines have experience with difficult guests." Marie's smile was thin. "Religious orders have their own reasons for opposing Nazi ideology."

As Marie prepared to melt back into the shadows, Marguerite called out one more question. "How long? How long has this network existed?"

"Since before the war began, in various forms. Your mother helped establish many of the connections we still use." Marie paused at the grove's edge. "She believed that resistance was like cultivating lavender —plant seeds early, tend them carefully, and eventually they bloom into something beautiful and enduring."

Then she was gone, leaving Marguerite alone with moonlight and the weight of inherited purpose. She sat for a long time among the ancient trees, trying to reconcile the mother she'd known with this hidden figure who'd built spy networks while teaching children their letters.

The walk back to the farm felt different, charged with new understanding and terrible responsibility. Tomorrow she would begin her masquerade as a collaborator, serving coffee to men who'd arrested her father while memorizing their conversations for transmission to the Resistance. The irony was bitter—protecting James by betraying everything she'd been taught about right and wrong.

But perhaps that was what her mother had understood all along. That in wartime, right and wrong became relative concepts, and survival sometimes required becoming someone else entirely.

She found Pierre waiting in the kitchen, young face etched with worry. "How did it go?"

"Marie will help extract James tomorrow night. And I'll be working at the mairie starting immediately—gathering intelligence for the Resistance." She watched his expression shift from relief to understanding to fear.

"You're going to spy on the Germans."

"I'm going to honor our mother's memory while trying to save our father's life." She gripped his hands, feeling the calluses that manual labor had carved into his palms. "But you stay clear of all this, understand? Focus on the farm, on rebuilding what we can. Let me handle the dangerous work."

"I'm not a child anymore, Marguerite. I could help—"

"You can help by surviving. By being here when this war ends, ready to plant lavender and rebuild our lives." Her voice broke slightly. "I've lost Maman, might lose Papa. I can't bear to lose you too."

He pulled her into a fierce embrace, and for a moment they were just orphaned siblings clinging together against the storm. When they separated, Pierre's jaw was set with determination that reminded her painfully of their father.

"All right. I'll be the innocent farm boy managing his inheritance. But if you need me—really need me—I'm here."

"I know." She managed a smile. "Now help me prepare for tomorrow. I have a role to perfect and a heart to break."

The next morning dawned grey and reluctant, matching her mood as she prepared for her first day at the mairie. She dressed with careful attention to detail—plain dark dress, severely braided hair, no cosmetics. The reflection in her mother's mirror showed a convincing portrait of rural desperation, someone too simple to threaten German efficiency.

Before leaving for the village, she made one last visit to James at the monastery. She found him in Brother Benedict's care, his color much improved though he still moved carefully to protect healing wounds.

"You look almost human again," she observed, settling beside his narrow bed.

"Feel it too, thanks to monastic hospitality and medical care." He caught her hand, studying her face with those impossibly blue eyes. "Something's changed. What's happened?"

She told him about Marie's revelations, the network's plans, her new role as reluctant spy. His expression grew increasingly grave as she spoke.

"You're going to work for the Germans while gathering intelligence for the Resistance," he said slowly. "That's... extraordinarily dangerous."

"Everything is dangerous now. At least this way I'm actively fighting back instead of simply hiding." She squeezed his fingers. "The extraction happens tonight. Marie's people will come for you after dark."

"And then I disappear into the network while you risk your life playing double agent." His free hand cupped her cheek. "This isn't how I wanted our story to end."

"It's not ending—it's pausing. There's a difference." She leaned into his touch, memorizing the warmth of his palm against her skin. "Besides, all the best stories have separation scenes. Adds dramatic tension."

"I hate dramatic tension. I prefer quiet domestic scenes with happy couples sharing breakfast." His thumb traced her cheekbone. "Promise me something?"

"What?"

"Don't lose yourself in this role. I've seen what happens to people who spend too long pretending to be someone else—the mask becomes the face." His blue eyes held fierce intensity. "Remember who you are beneath whatever performance you have to give."

"I'll remember." She kissed his palm, tasting salt and soap and the faint antiseptic smell from his bandages. "And you remember to stay alive. When this war ends—and it will end—I'm coming back. I'll find you, Marguerite Dubois, and court you properly."

The words hung between them like a bridge across impossible distance. She wanted to believe in that future, in Sunday afternoon walks and proper courtship and all the time in the world to love each other without fear.

"That's a beautiful dream," she whispered.

"It's not a dream—it's a promise." He pulled her closer, kissing her with desperate tenderness. "I love you, Marguerite. I know it's too soon, too complicated, too everything. But I needed to say it once, clearly, so you'll carry it with you."

"James—"

"You don't have to say it back. Just remember that you're loved. When the weight of secrets becomes unbearable, when playing your role feels like betraying your soul, remember that someone loves you exactly as you are."

She kissed him instead of answering, trying to pour a lifetime of feelings into the contact. When they parted, both were breathing hard, both fighting tears.

"I should go," she said without moving. "The mairie expects their new clerk promptly at eight."

"Then go. Play your part. Save your father. Show those Nazi bastards that French women are forces of nature disguised as flowers."

She left before her resolve could crumble, walking through morning mist toward the village and her new life as a double agent. The mairie loomed ahead with its swastika banner hanging limp in the still air, and she steeled herself for the performance of a lifetime.

Invisibility as armor, Marie had said. The lesson her mother had taught without words, the legacy passed from one generation of secret fighters to the next. Marguerite Dubois was about to disappear, replaced by a simple farm girl grateful for German employment.

But beneath the mask, the real woman would endure. Would remember love and lavender fields and the promise of pilots returning. Would gather secrets like her mother before her, turning information into weapons against tyranny.

The resistance lived in ordinary people doing extraordinary things.

In teachers who memorized conversations, in farmers who hid pilots, in daughters who honored their parents' hidden courage.

In women who learned that sometimes the greatest act of defiance was to smile while serving coffee to the enemy, all while planning their destruction from within.

The ancient olive grove held its secrets, but it had witnessed the birth of another. Tonight, James would disappear into the network that might carry him home. Tomorrow, Marguerite would begin the dangerous work of becoming invisible while gathering the intelligence that might save her father and serve her country.

The war continued, but the players were changing. And sometimes, that was how victories began—with quiet women accepting dangerous legacies, one carefully memorized conversation at a time.

❧ 6 ❧

THE FIRST MISSION

Three weeks had passed since James's extraction, three weeks of careful performance at the mairie while Marguerite gathered intelligence like gleaning wheat—one precious grain at a time. September had arrived with unusual heat, turning the lavender fields bronze at their edges and making the German soldiers irritable in their wool uniforms. The rhythm of her double life had become as natural as breathing: rise before dawn to tend the farm, present herself at the mairie as the grateful, simple farm girl, serve coffee and file papers while memorizing every conversation, every document, every carelessly spoken detail.

The role fit her like a second skin now. Madame Pelletier treated her with maternal kindness, the German officers looked through her as if she were furniture, and Captain Weiss observed her with the casual attention one might give a moderately interesting insect. Perfect invisibility, just as her mother had taught her without words.

This morning brought unusual tension to the administrative offices. Officers clustered around maps with voices pitched low but urgent, their movements sharp with purpose. Something significant was building—she could feel it in the increased security, the way even routine documents were suddenly classified, the brittle energy that preceded major operations.

"Girl! Coffee!" Lieutenant Krause barked from the conference room, his usual bored authority replaced by tight focus.

"Yes, sir. Right away, sir." She scurried to comply, silver tray balanced carefully as she entered the room where destiny was being planned.

The conference table held maps of the coastal region, red circles marking locations she recognized—the old mill at Rastoul where everyone knew Resistance fighters gathered, the abandoned quarry near Forcalquier, the farmhouse at Les Baux that had been suspiciously active lately. Times were marked beside each circle: 0200, 0215, 0230.

"Careful with that pot," Captain Weiss said mildly as she poured, though his pale eyes watched her with their usual calculated suspicion. "Wouldn't want any accidents."

"No, sir. Sorry, sir." She affected nervous clumsiness, nearly dropping the sugar bowl while her mind photographed every visible detail. Coordinated raids, precisely timed, three locations that housed Resistance activities. The kind of operation that could decapitate the regional network in a single night.

"The transport arrangements?" Major Holz was asking, his finger tracing routes on the map.

"Confirmed. Prisoner trucks will be positioned here and here." Lieutenant Weber indicated staging areas. "Estimate capacity for forty detainees per location, assuming standard resistance cell composition."

Forty detainees. Her blood chilled as the mathematics became clear. They weren't planning arrests—they were planning a massacre disguised as law enforcement.

"Excellent." Weiss's smile was winter-sharp. "Operation Mistral will demonstrate the futility of resistance activities in this region. Coordinated strikes, simultaneous timing, no opportunity for warnings between cells."

"Coffee, mein Herr?" She approached Major Holz with steady hands despite her racing heart.

"Ja, danke." He barely glanced at her, already turning back to the maps. "The communication blackout is confirmed? No radio traffic, no telephone connections?"

"All arranged. Starting at midnight, all civilian communications will be severed until operations complete." Weber consulted his notes. "The terrorists will be isolated, unable to coordinate escape or resistance."

She finished serving and retreated to her desk, mind racing through implications. A coordinated assault on three Resistance strongholds, timed to prevent warnings, supported by communication blackouts and overwhelming force. Marie's network faced annihilation unless someone could warn them. Unless someone who served coffee and filed papers and had learned to be invisible could find a way to sound the alarm.

The morning crawled past with agonizing slowness. She transcribed correspondence with mechanical precision while her thoughts churned through possibilities. How to contact Marie without arousing suspicion? How to warn three separate cells without access to normal communication channels? How to save lives when every hour of delay potentially cost them?

The answer came through German efficiency itself. A supply requisition crossed her desk, routine paperwork for "additional medical supplies for prisoner interrogation following Operation Mistral." The euphemistic language couldn't disguise the reality—they expected wounded prisoners, lots of them. This wasn't just arrest and imprisonment; it was systematic brutality designed to break the Resistance through terror.

Her hands trembled as she filed the document, fury mixing with fear. These men spoke casually of torture while drinking coffee she'd served, planning atrocities with the same attention they'd give crop rotation schedules. But fury was useful—it burned away hesitation and crystallized purpose. She would find a way to warn the network. She had to.

At lunch, she claimed female troubles requiring a visit to the pharmacist—a perfectly reasonable excuse that made the German soldiers uncomfortable enough to avoid questions. Instead of the pharmacy, she slipped into the church where Father Auguste waited in his confessional, deaf enough to provide perfect cover for clandestine conversations.

"Bless me, Father, for I have urgent news," she whispered through the screen.

"Speak up, child. These old ears..." The priest's voice carried its usual confusion, but his eyes were sharp with understanding.

"Operation Mistral. Tonight at two in the morning. Coordinated raids on three locations: Rastoul mill, Forcalquier quarry, Les Baux farmhouse. Communication blackout starting at midnight. Prisoner trucks, interrogation supplies—they're planning complete destruction of regional cells."

Father Auguste absorbed this with remarkable calm for a supposedly senile old man. "Marie should know this immediately. Can you reach her?"

"Not without arousing suspicion. I'm expected back at the mairie within the hour."

"Leave that to me. Return to your duties. Act normally. If anyone asks, you consulted me about your mother's memorial service—perfectly innocent." His weathered hand made the sign of blessing. "Go with God, child. And know that your courage serves Heaven's purpose."

The afternoon felt endless. She filed papers and served refreshments while watching the clock's hands crawl toward evening. Every German officer who glanced her way sent ice through her veins. Did they suspect? Had someone noticed her extended lunch? Was this elaborate surveillance designed to expose her?

But paranoia was a luxury she couldn't afford. At five o'clock, Madame Pelletier dismissed her with the same maternal kindness as always. No extra guards, no searching questions, no sign that her morning's intelligence gathering had been detected. The Germans' arrogance was their weakness—they couldn't imagine that the simple farm girl who served their coffee might be memorizing their battle plans.

The walk home felt surreal, everyday sights overlaid with approaching catastrophe. She found Pierre repairing the chicken coop, shirt soaked with honest sweat, completely unaware that tonight would determine the Resistance's survival in their region.

"You're late," he said without looking up. "Everything all right at the mairie?"

"Fine. Just extra filing." She hated lying to him but saw no alternative. The less he knew, the safer he remained. "I'm exhausted—might go to bed early."

"You've been saying that a lot lately." He studied her with eyes too knowing for seventeen. "Whatever you're doing for Marie, be careful. The Germans have been more active lately—more patrols, more searches. Something has them stirred up."

If only he knew how stirred up they'd be by tomorrow morning. But she managed a tired smile. "Just gathering information, nothing dangerous. Though you're right about the increased patrols. We should keep a low profile for a while."

Dinner was a quiet affair, both lost in their thoughts. She went to bed at her usual time, waiting for Pierre's breathing to deepen into sleep before rising and dressing in dark clothes. At eleven o'clock, she slipped out through the kitchen window—if the Germans were watching, they'd expect her to use doors like a normal person.

The church stood empty in the moonlight, but Marie waited in the vestry as Father Auguste had promised. The older woman's face was grave with received intelligence.

"Three hours," Marie said without preamble. "Can it be done?"

"The mill and quarry, yes. They're close enough for fast travel. But Les Baux is fifteen kilometers—even with motorcycles, the timing is impossible."

"Then we save who we can and mourn the rest." Marie's matter-of-fact tone couldn't disguise the pain beneath. "Though perhaps... do you remember the communication blackout starts at midnight?"

"Yes. No radio or telephone traffic until operations complete."

"Blackouts work both ways. If German communications are severed, their coordination fails too." Marie's smile was sharp as a blade. "We have assets inside the telephone exchange. A little sabotage, some misdirected orders, confusion about timing and targets..."

"You can turn their own plan against them?"

"We can try. Your intelligence gives us the gift of preparation—now we'll see if preparation can bloom into victory." Marie gripped her shoulders. "This is your first real success, child. You've potentially saved dozens of lives tonight."

"If the plan works."

"If it doesn't, at least our people will die fighting instead of sleeping. Sometimes that's the most we can hope for." Marie moved toward the door. "Return home. Maintain normal patterns. If anyone asks, you never left your bed."

But Marguerite couldn't simply return home and wait for news. She'd discovered the threat, transmitted the warning—now she needed to know if her efforts had saved lives or merely delayed slaughter. Instead of heading directly back to the farm, she took the longer route through the hills that would let her observe the Rastoul mill from a distance.

She reached the overlook at one-thirty, thirty minutes before the planned assault. The mill stood dark and seemingly abandoned in the valley below, its ancient stones giving no hint of whether the warning had arrived in time. German vehicles were already moving into position—she could see their shrouded headlights converging on approach roads.

At exactly two o'clock, the assault began. Floodlights blazed to life, illuminating empty buildings as German soldiers charged through doorways and windows with military precision. Shouts echoed through the valley—orders, confusion, growing frustration as the raids found nothing but abandoned meeting spaces and cold cooking fires.

From her concealed position, Marguerite watched the operation unravel. Radio chatter crackled through the night air, voices growing increasingly agitated as reports came in from the other locations. Empty. All empty. Coordinated evacuations that suggested advance warning, counter-preparations that turned German organization against itself.

"Verflucht!" A German officer's curse carried clearly in the still air. "How did they know?"

The raids continued for another hour, soldiers searching every stone, every shadow, finding nothing but evidence of hasty abandonment. As dawn approached, the forces withdrew with visible frustration, their perfect operation transformed into public failure.

Marguerite made her way home as the first grey light touched the mountains, exhaustion and relief making her legs unsteady. She'd done it—discovered the plan, transmitted the warning, watched her intelligence bloom into salvation for dozens of Resistance fighters. Her first real mission had succeeded beyond her wildest hopes.

Pierre was waiting in the kitchen when she slipped back through the window, young face grave with worry. "Where were you?"

"Restless night. Walked to clear my head." Another lie, but a necessary one. "Did you hear anything? Sounds from the valley?"

"Some commotion near Rastoul. Vehicles, shouting. Probably German exercises." He studied her carefully. "You don't seem surprised."

"Nothing surprises me anymore. The Germans do what they do, we endure what we must." She managed a tired smile. "Now I really do need sleep. Wake me if anyone comes asking questions."

But sleep wouldn't come. Her mind replayed the night's events—the discovery, the warning, the empty buildings that had saved so many lives. She'd crossed another threshold, from passive observer to active savior. The weight of it settled into her bones, both burden and blessing.

Three days later, as she served morning coffee at the mairie, the full scope of their success became clear. Captain Weiss's face was thunderous as he read reports from the failed operation, his pale eyes scanning the room as if German efficiency itself had betrayed him.

"Sabotage," he announced to the gathered officers. "Coordinated information leaks, communication disruptions, systematic warnings delivered to terrorist cells. Someone in this region is feeding intelligence to the Resistance."

"All three locations were evacuated," Major Holz reported with visible frustration. "Clean withdrawals, no equipment left behind, no traces of where they've relocated. Professional work."

"Too professional," Weiss agreed. "This wasn't lucky guesswork. Someone with access to operational planning provided specific warnings." His gaze swept the room, lingering on each face with calculated suspicion. "Find them. I want investigations into every civilian employee, every local contact, every possible source of contamination."

Marguerite kept her expression carefully neutral while serving fresh coffee, projecting the mild interest of a simple farm girl learning about important events. Inside, pride warred with terror. She'd dealt the local German command a significant defeat, but victory carried its own dangers. Increased scrutiny, deeper investigations, the very success that proved her value also made her more vulnerable to exposure.

"Will there be anything else, sir?" she asked as she finished serving.

"No, that will be all," Weiss replied curtly, his attention already returned to the maps and reports. The simple farm girl who served coffee had earned no more notice than the furniture.

She retreated to her desk with careful composure, mind racing through implications. Her first major intelligence coup had succeeded beyond expectations, but it also marked her transition from passive observer to active threat to German operations. The work would only grow more dangerous from here.

That evening, she met Marie at their usual rendezvous in the olive grove. The older woman's face lit up with satisfaction as Marguerite reported the aftermath of the failed raids.

"Magnificent work," Marie said with genuine warmth. "Not just the intelligence gathering, but the courage to act on it immediately. You saved at least thirty lives that night, possibly more."

"And exposed myself in the process. Weiss is suspicious of everyone now, investigating all civilian contacts."

"Suspicion without evidence is manageable. Continue your performance, maintain your cover identity. The simple farm girl role has served you well." Marie's eyes gleamed with professional interest. "Your success demonstrates capability beyond simple intelligence gathering. I'm officially appointing you as chief intelligence coordinator for the coastal region."

The title hit like a physical blow. "Chief coordinator? But I'm barely trained, just started active operations—"

"You're trained by necessity, tested by fire, and proven by results. The coastal region needs someone who can build networks, coordinate information flows, manage multiple assets." Marie's voice carried absolute certainty. "Your mother prepared you for this role without either of you knowing it. Now it's time to embrace that preparation."

"There's something else." Marguerite reached into her pocket, withdrawing a small piece of paper. "This came through the BBC yesterday evening. I think you should hear it."

Marie examined the transcribed message by moonlight. "The Yorkshire rose is warming in the Spanish sun. Repeat—the Yorkshire rose is warming in the Spanish sun." Understanding dawned on her weathered features. "Your pilot. He's reached Spain."

"James made it across the border." The words carried relief mixed with longing. He was beyond German reach, but also further from any possibility of return. "The network succeeded."

"As did you. Your intelligence gathered in those first weeks, your careful maintenance of his health, your willingness to accept danger for his sake—all of that contributed to his successful extraction." Marie folded the message carefully. "He owes his life to your courage."

"And I owe my purpose to his presence. Strange how these things balance."

"Not strange—necessary. War creates connections we'd never imagine in peacetime, forces us to discover strength we didn't know we possessed." Marie stood, preparing to leave. "Speaking of which, your success with Operation Mistral demonstrates capability beyond simple intelligence gathering. I'm officially appointing you as chief intelligence coordinator for the coastal region."

The title hit like a physical blow. "Chief coordinator? But I'm barely trained, just started active operations—"

"You're trained by necessity, tested by fire, and proven by results. The coastal region needs someone who can build networks, coordinate information flows, manage multiple assets." Marie's voice carried absolute certainty. "Your mother prepared you for this role without either of you knowing it. Now it's time to embrace that preparation."

"What does it mean, practically?"

"You'll recruit informants—carefully, slowly, people with access to different aspects of German operations. Coordinate intelligence between cells, ensuring information reaches those who can act on it.

Manage security protocols, identify threats before they become crises." Marie paused meaningfully. "And plan operations based on gathered intelligence. Not just warning about German plans, but creating our own."

The scope was overwhelming. From serving coffee and filing papers to coordinating regional resistance activities in the space of a few weeks. But she thought of those empty buildings at Rastoul, of lives saved by timely warnings, of James safely extracted to continue fighting from England.

"I accept," she said quietly. "What do I need to know?"

They talked until dawn, Marie outlining networks and procedures, contact protocols and security measures. Marguerite absorbed it all— the weight of responsibility, the complexity of coordination, the constant danger that came with leadership. By the time they parted, she understood both the opportunity and the burden she'd accepted.

The walk home took her past lavender fields touched with morning light, their purple blooms holding steady despite the storms raging around them. Like the flowers, she would endure, would bloom when conditions allowed, would spread her roots deep enough to survive whatever came.

At the farm, Pierre was already working in the vegetable garden, proving himself the competent caretaker she'd hoped he'd become. He looked up as she approached, noting her expression with growing understanding.

"More responsibilities?" he asked without preamble.

"Many more. I'll be traveling occasionally, meeting with contacts, coordinating activities beyond just gathering intelligence." She sat beside him on the garden wall. "Can you manage the farm alone when needed?"

"I've been managing it alone for weeks already," he pointed out. "You've been too busy playing spy to notice the harvest coming in perfectly well without you."

The gentle reproach stung because it was accurate. Her Resistance work had consumed more attention than she'd realized, pulling her away from the farm that had always been her foundation.

"I'm sorry. I know I've been distracted—"

"You've been saving lives," he interrupted. "I'm proud of what you're doing, even if I worry constantly about losing you too." His young face was serious. "Just remember that the farm will be here when the war ends. We'll need something to rebuild on."

"I'll remember." She gripped his hand, drawing strength from his steady presence. "And Pierre? If anyone asks—anyone at all—you know nothing about my activities. I work at the mairie, keep house, manage the farm. Nothing more complicated than that."

"I've been practicing ignorance for weeks," he said dryly. "I'm becoming quite expert at it."

Monday morning brought her introduction to Lieutenant Weber and her new position in intelligence coordination. The work was indeed more interesting—actual documents instead of overheard conversations, operational files instead of casual gossip, systematic analysis instead of random observation.

And more dangerous. Weber was sharp where other officers were complacent, suspicious where they were dismissive. He watched her work with professional attention, testing her responses, measuring her reactions. The promotion she'd celebrated might become the trap that exposed her.

But she'd crossed too many lines to retreat now. The chief intelligence coordinator for the coastal region had work to do—networks to build, operations to plan, a war to win one carefully gathered secret at a time.

The lavender fields outside the mairie windows held their ancient promise of endurance and renewal. James was safe in England, her father endured in his prison, the Resistance had survived its first major test. It was enough to build on, enough to hope on.

The real work was just beginning.

❦

7

THE WEIGHT OF ABSENCE

NOVEMBER 1942

T he mountain safe house perched like an eagle's nest among bare limestone peaks, its stone walls weathered by centuries of mistral winds and countless secrets. November had settled over the Luberon with unusual severity, turning the valleys below into a monochrome tapestry of frost-blackened vines and skeletal plane trees. From the narrow window of her temporary quarters, Marguerite watched clouds gather above peaks that had sheltered refugees and resistants since Roman times.

Two months had passed since James's extraction, two months of careful numbness wrapped around a secret that grew heavier each day. She pressed her palm against her still-flat stomach, feeling the changes her body insisted upon despite her mind's refusal to accept them. Three months along, conceived in those stolen August nights when love had bloomed amid lavender and borrowed time.

Pregnant. The word sat in her consciousness like a stone, immovable and transformative. In peacetime, it might have been cause for celebration, for careful planning and joyful anticipation. In wartime, carrying an enemy pilot's child while coordinating regional resistance operations, it was a complication that could destroy everything she'd built.

"You're pushing yourself too hard," Pierre observed from the doorway, his young face etched with concern that had aged him beyond his eighteen years. He'd grown into someone who commanded respect from men twice his age, shoulders broadened by months of managing both farm and family responsibilities. "When did you last sleep more than three hours?"

"Sleep is a luxury," she replied, not turning from the window. Below in the courtyard, resistance fighters cleaned weapons and studied maps, preparing for operations that might never return them to these mountains. "The network requires constant coordination."

"The network requires you functional, not collapsed from exhaustion." He entered the room, noting the way she held herself—careful, protective, subtly different. "Marguerite, what's wrong? Really wrong, not this surface exhaustion."

She wanted to tell him, to share the burden that pressed against her ribs like trapped breath. But Pierre had enough to carry without adding her impossible situation to his load. The secret pregnancy was another weight to bear alone, another performance to maintain.

"Nothing's wrong beyond the usual impossibilities." She managed a tired smile. "Marie's planning expanded operations, London wants detailed coastal intelligence, and our contact networks need constant maintenance. It's demanding work."

"But important work." His eyes searched her face with uncomfortable perception. "Still, even the most important work can't sustain someone who's running on air and stubbornness."

Before she could deflect further, boots rang on stone stairs. Marie Beaumont appeared in the doorway, her weathered face grave with the kind of news that had become too familiar.

"We have a problem," she announced without preamble. "The third parachute drop this month was intercepted. Complete German ambush—supplies lost, three agents captured."

Marguerite felt ice settle in her stomach. "That's not coincidence."

"No, it's betrayal. Someone with access to our operational schedules is feeding information to the Germans." Marie entered the room, closing the door behind her. "Three drops, three interceptions. Perfect timing, precise locations. They're not guessing."

The implications rippled outward like stone thrown in still water. Their network, carefully built over months of patient recruitment, had been penetrated. Someone they trusted was selling lives for German favor or German threats.

"How many people knew the drop schedules?" Pierre asked, his voice tight with the kind of anger that comes from violated trust.

"Too many. Operations this size require coordination between multiple cells—timing, location security, transport arrangements." Marie pulled out a worn map, marking the intercepted drops with red ink. "The Germans knew exactly when and where to wait. Professional intelligence, not lucky patrol work."

Marguerite studied the pattern, mind working through networks and connections with mechanical precision. The pregnancy's constant nausea made concentration difficult, but this required her full attention. Lives depended on identifying the leak before more operations were compromised.

"The London supplies are critical," she said, thinking of the medical equipment, radio components, and weapons that had been lost. "Without regular drops, the regional cells can't maintain effectiveness."

"Worse than that," Marie replied grimly. "London is considering suspending all supply operations to our sector until the security breach is identified. That would cripple resistance activities just as German pressure is increasing."

The meeting was interrupted by soft knocking—the coded rhythm that meant urgent message traffic. Pierre answered to find Dr. Bernard, his medical bag suggesting either wounded fighters or sensitive communications that required face-to-face delivery.

"From London," he said quietly, producing a sealed envelope from his bag's false bottom. "Came through the diplomatic channels via Switzerland."

Marie opened it with careful hands, reading the decoded message with increasing satisfaction. "Finally, some good news. 'The Yorkshire rose has been replanted in English soil and shows signs of healthy growth. Gardener reports excellent adaptation to Scottish climate and specialized training regimen.'"

Marguerite's heart leaped despite the careful coded language. James —alive, safe, recovered from his escape ordeal. More than that, if the message was accurate: "Scottish climate and specialized training regimen" could only mean one thing.

"SOE," she breathed. "He's training with the Special Operations Executive."

"Appears so. Specialized training for agents being dropped back into occupied territory." Marie's smile was sharp with professional approval. "Your pilot is being prepared to return as something more than a downed airman."

The news hit like physical force. James was safe, but he was also being trained to return to France—to the same dangers that had nearly killed him during his first visit. The joy of knowing he lived warred with terror at the thought of him parachuting back into German-occupied territory.

"When?" she asked, surprised by the steadiness of her own voice.

"Unknown. SOE training takes months, sometimes longer. Could be spring before he's operational." Marie studied Marguerite's face with uncomfortable perception. "How do you feel about that possibility?"

How did she feel? Relief that he lived, terror that he'd return, joy at the thought of seeing him again, panic at the impossibility of explaining a pregnancy conceived during his first visit. The emotions tangled into something too complex for simple answers.

"I feel like a professional intelligence coordinator who understands operational necessities," she replied carefully. "Personal feelings don't alter strategic requirements."

"Very diplomatic." But Marie's expression suggested she wasn't fooled by the professional facade. "We'll cross that bridge when we reach it. For now, our immediate concern is identifying the traitor before more lives are lost."

They spent the afternoon analyzing patterns, comparing operational timelines with personnel access. The exercise was both methodical and heartbreaking—reducing trusted colleagues to suspects based on opportunity and access. But someone in their network was selling intelligence that got agents killed, and sentiment couldn't protect betrayers.

"Here," Pierre said, pointing to a name on their organizational chart. "René Duclos. He had access to all three drop schedules, helped coordinate ground security for each operation."

"René's been with us since the beginning," Marie protested. "His brother was shot by the Germans, his farm requisitioned for military use. Why would he collaborate?"

"Maybe they threatened what family he has left. Maybe they offered enough money to matter. Maybe they simply broke him." Marguerite studied the pattern with cold professional attention. "Motivation matters less than capability and access."

The analysis continued as darkness fell, oil lamps casting shifting shadows across maps and personnel files. Marguerite fought waves of nausea that pregnancy brought with increasing frequency, disguising them as exhaustion from the long day. The secret pressed against her consciousness like physical weight—how long before it became impossible to hide?

"We need verification before acting," Marie decided finally. "False accusations destroy networks as effectively as real betrayal. I'll arrange a test—false information about a fictional drop, see if it reaches German ears."

"And if René is the traitor?"

"Then we deal with him according to resistance protocols." Marie's voice carried the cold finality of someone who'd made such decisions before. "Betrayal in wartime carries only one sentence."

That evening, Marguerite walked alone among the bare chestnut groves that surrounded their mountain refuge. The November air cut through her coat with knife-edge clarity, carrying scents of wood smoke and approaching snow. She needed solitude to process the day's revelations—James's safety and training, the network's betrayal, the pregnancy that complicated everything.

At a clearing overlooking the valley, she stopped to rest on a fallen log. Below, scattered lights marked villages that had endured occupation for over two years, their inhabitants adapting to survive. Like the pregnancy growing inside her—an adaptation to circumstances beyond her control, requiring resources she wasn't sure she possessed.

"The symptoms will get worse before they get better."

She spun to find Dr. Bernard approaching through the trees, his medical bag suggesting this wasn't coincidental encounter.

"I don't know what you mean," she said carefully.

"The morning sickness, fatigue, emotional sensitivity. Classic signs of early pregnancy, though you're hiding them well." His weathered face held paternal kindness mixed with professional concern. "How far along?"

For a moment, she considered maintaining the pretense. But secrets had weight, and she was already carrying too many.

"Three months. Conceived in late August." The admission felt like physical relief, sharing the burden she'd carried alone. "I haven't told anyone, not even Pierre."

"The pilot's child," Bernard said without judgment. "Complications aside, are you well? Any bleeding, severe pain?"

"No complications. Just the usual symptoms." She managed a bitter laugh. "Though 'usual' takes on different meaning when you're coordinating resistance operations while hiding pregnancy."

"Have you considered options? It's not too late for medical intervention, if that's your choice."

She'd considered everything—abortion, adoption, attempting to raise a war baby alone. None of the options offered easy solutions.

"I've considered. But ending it feels like... killing the only part of James I'll have if he doesn't survive the war." She pressed her palm to her stomach again. "And keeping it means explaining a pregnancy without a husband, raising a child while fighting an occupation."

"Women have managed both throughout history," Bernard said gently. "Though never easily."

"What would you advise?"

"I'd advise telling Pierre. He's stronger than you credit, and family secrets have a way of emerging at inconvenient times." The doctor stood, preparing to leave. "Also, consider that the child might be a gift rather than a complication. War takes so much—perhaps this is life's way of balancing accounts."

After he left, Marguerite sat alone with November darkness and impossible choices. The pregnancy was real, undeniable, growing despite her fears and complications. James was alive but training for missions that might kill him. The resistance network she'd helped build was compromised by betrayal from within.

The weight of absence pressed down like the cold mountain air— James's physical absence, her father's continued imprisonment, her mother's death that had started this chain of impossible choices. But absence also created space for growth, for the kind of strength that could only develop when support was stripped away.

She thought of lavender fields waiting dormant through winter, roots deep enough to survive the worst weather. The plants knew how to endure seasons that would kill weaker species, how to bloom again when conditions allowed. Perhaps she could learn the same patience, the same stubborn endurance that turned survival into eventual victory.

The walk back to the safe house took her past sentries who nodded recognition, past windows where resistance fighters planned operations that would shape the war's direction. She belonged here among these people who'd chosen danger over safety, principle over comfort. The pregnancy would complicate that belonging, but it wouldn't end it.

In her quarters, she found Pierre waiting with hot tea and worried expression.

"Better?" he asked, noting her improved color.

"Better," she agreed, though better was relative in wartime. "Pierre, there's something I need to tell you. Something important."

He set down his cup, giving her full attention with the patience he'd learned from managing crises. At eighteen, he'd become someone who could bear difficult news without flinching.

"I'm pregnant," she said simply. "Three months along. James's child."

For a moment, Pierre was perfectly still. Then his face cycled through surprise, understanding, concern, and finally determination.

"All right," he said calmly. "What do we need to do?"

The simple acceptance nearly undid her careful composure. No judgment, no questions about impossibilities or complications—just immediate focus on practical requirements.

"I don't know yet. I'm still deciding what's possible." She gripped his hands. "But I needed you to know, needed someone to share the weight."

"You don't have to carry anything alone," he said firmly. "We're family. We face whatever comes together."

"Even when what comes is a war baby with an absent father and a mother who spends her time coordinating dangerous operations?"

"Especially then." His smile held the warmth that had sustained them through their mother's death and father's imprisonment. "Though we might need to discuss operational modifications as you get further along."

That night, for the first time in weeks, Marguerite slept deeply. The secret was shared, the burden lightened by Pierre's steady acceptance. James was alive and training, the network's betrayal would be addressed, and the pregnancy would be managed like every other wartime challenge—with patience, planning, and stubborn determination to survive.

The weight of absence remained, but it no longer crushed. Instead, it had become foundation for something new—the knowledge that love could create life even in wartime's darkest moments, that hope could grow in the most impossible soil.

Outside, November wind rattled shutters and scattered the last leaves from mountain oaks. Winter was coming, but spring would follow. The lavender fields would bloom again, and perhaps by then, the world would be different enough to welcome new life safely.

She placed her hand on her stomach, feeling the future growing there despite everything trying to prevent it. A child conceived in love and hope, carried through danger and uncertainty, destined to be born into whatever world their resistance could help create.

It was enough to hope on. It had to be.

✿

❧ 8 ❧

LOVE IN WARTIME

DECEMBER 1942

The message arrived on a bitter December morning when frost turned the mountain pines into silver sentinels. Marguerite studied the coded paper Marie had pressed into her hands, her breath forming white clouds in the frigid air of the cave that served as their command post. Four months of pregnancy had rounded her face slightly, softened the sharp angles that two years of occupation had carved there, but her eyes remained steel.

"Four days," she said, the words dropping like stones into the silence.

Around the rough wooden table, faces turned toward her—weathered, scarred faces that had learned to read death in the spaces between words. Marie's expression remained carefully neutral, but Claude shifted his weight, the movement sending his rifle strap sliding against stone.

"Four days until the transport leaves Marseille," Marguerite continued, her voice steady despite the tremor in her hands. "Henri Dubois, prisoner number 4,847, scheduled for transfer to Mauthausen labor camp."

Pierre's sharp intake of breath cut through the cave's stillness. At seventeen, he had grown tall and lean, his boyish features hardened by months of living rough in the mountains. But now, hearing his father's name spoken like an inventory item, he looked suddenly young again.

"We have to get him out." The words escaped him in a rush, desperate and raw.

"Sit down." Marie's command was quiet but absolute. "This isn't a decision made with hearts."

But Pierre remained standing, his hands curled into fists at his sides. "He's my father."

"He's all our fathers." Claude's gravelly voice carried the weight of his sixty years, each one etched in the deep lines around his eyes. "Every man they've taken, every woman, every child. But sentiment doesn't stop bullets, boy."

Marguerite watched her brother's face cycle through emotions— anger, hurt, determination. In the wavering candlelight, she could see echoes of the child who used to chase butterflies through the lavender fields, but also glimpses of the man he was becoming. The man this war was forcing him to become.

"Tell us what you know," she said to Marie, settling her hand protectively over the slight curve of her belly. The baby stirred, a flutter of movement that still amazed her, even as it complicated everything.

Marie spread a hand-drawn map across the table's scarred surface. "The transport leaves Fort Saint-Nicolas at dawn on December fifteenth. Forty-three prisoners, twelve guards, two trucks. They'll take the coastal road to Toulon, then north through the mountains."

"Forty-three." Marguerite traced the route with her finger, calculating distances, timing, variables. "How many are ours?"

"Seven confirmed resistance. Maybe three more sympathizers." Marie's finger tapped specific points along the route. "The convoy will be most vulnerable here, in the Maurel Pass. Steep drops on both sides, limited visibility, nowhere to call for reinforcements."

"Perfect for an ambush," Claude murmured, leaning closer to study the terrain. "But also perfect for a massacre if we get it wrong."

Silence stretched between them, thick with unspoken calculations.

Marguerite felt the weight of leadership settling on her shoulders like a yoke. Every face around this table would look to her for the final decision. Every life risked would be her responsibility.

"What assets do we have?" she asked.

"Fifteen fighters," Marie replied promptly. "Three Sten guns, assorted rifles, enough ammunition for maybe twenty minutes of serious fighting. No explosives—the last drop was intercepted."

"Fifteen against twelve, plus whatever backup they might call." Marguerite's mind worked through the mathematics of warfare, the cold calculations that had kept them alive this long. "Poor odds."

"I'm going." Pierre's voice cut through their tactical discussion, firm and unwavering.

"You're staying here." Marguerite didn't look up from the map. "End of discussion."

"Like hell I am." Pierre's hand slammed against the table, making the candles jump. "I've been training for months. I know how to handle weapons, how to move quietly, how to—"

"How to get yourself killed." Marguerite finally raised her eyes to meet his. "Or worse, get everyone else killed trying to protect you."

"I'm not a child anymore!" The words exploded from him, echoing off the cave walls. "I've earned the right to fight for my father."

"Rights?" Claude's laugh was bitter. "There are no rights in war, boy. Only responsibilities. And right now, your responsibility is to survive. Someone needs to carry on the family name if this goes to hell."

Pierre's face flushed red in the flickering light. "So I'm supposed to hide in the mountains while strangers risk their lives for my father?"

"Yes." Marguerite's answer was immediate and final. "That's exactly what you're supposed to do."

But even as she said it, she could see the rebellion building in her brother's eyes, the stubborn set of his jaw that marked him as Henri's son. This was the boy who had helped their mother hide Jewish children, who had kept that secret even from his father. This was the young man who had proven himself in countless small operations, who had saved lives and taken risks with a maturity that belied his years.

Marie cleared her throat delicately. "Perhaps we should focus on the operational details first. Family dynamics can be resolved after we have a plan."

Marguerite nodded, grateful for the reprieve. "Walk us through it."

"Two teams," Marie began, her finger tracing positions on the map. "One here, at the northern end of the pass, to stop the convoy. The other here, at the southern approach, to prevent retreat or reinforcement."

"Crossfire," Claude observed. "Our people will be caught in the middle."

"Only if they're still on the trucks. The plan is to stop the convoy, eliminate the guards quickly, then extract our people before German reinforcements arrive."

"How long do we have?" Marguerite asked.

"From the moment shooting starts? Maybe fifteen minutes before the nearest German garrison realizes something's wrong. Twenty minutes until they arrive in force."

"Fifteen minutes to save forty-three lives." Marguerite sat back, one hand absently rubbing her belly as the baby kicked. "And if we fail?"

"If we fail, we lose some of the best resistance fighters in the region. And they lose their last chance at freedom."

The weight of that truth settled over the cave like a shroud. Marguerite looked around the table at faces she had learned to read like family—Marie's careful composure hiding deep wells of grief for comrades already lost; Claude's gruff exterior masking a heart that bled for every injustice; Pierre's desperate love for a father he might never see again.

"I want to go over the timeline again," she said finally. "Every detail, every contingency. If we're going to do this, we do it right."

For the next hour, they dissected the plan with surgical precision. Guard rotations, weapon assignments, escape routes, fallback positions. Marguerite found herself thinking in the clipped, tactical language that had become second nature—approach vectors and fields of fire, ammunition expenditure and casualty estimates.

But underneath the professional discussion, her heart hammered with more personal fears. Four months pregnant, she could still fight if necessary, but her balance was already changing, her reflexes slightly slower. More critically, she carried the future of the Dubois line in her womb—James's child, the grandchild Henri had never met.

What right did she have to risk that future for the sake of one rescue, no matter how personal?

What right did she have not to?

"I still think we need more fighters," Claude was saying. "Fifteen is barely enough, and that's assuming everything goes perfectly."

"Everything never goes perfectly," Marie replied dryly. "We work with what we have."

"What about the Lyon cell?" Pierre interjected. "They owe us for the ammunition we shared last month."

"Three days' travel, minimum," Marguerite said. "We don't have time."

"Then we make it work with fifteen." Claude's voice carried the resignation of a man who had seen too many impossible odds. "Wouldn't be the first time."

As they refined details and assigned positions, Marguerite found her mind drifting to James, somewhere in Scotland learning the deadly skills of the Special Operations Executive. Did he think of her in the brief moments between training exercises? Did he wonder if he would ever see his child?

A coded BBC message two weeks ago had confirmed his safe arrival: "The Yorkshire rose has been replanted in English soil." But that had been their last contact. For all she knew, he was already dead, killed in some training accident or preliminary mission.

The thought sent a chill through her that had nothing to do with the December cold.

"Marguerite?" Marie's voice cut through her distraction. "We need your decision."

All eyes were on her again—waiting, trusting, believing she could somehow make the impossible choice between family and duty, love and survival. Outside the cave, wind howled through the pines like the voices of the dead, reminding her of every friend already lost to this war.

Henri had been gone four months. Four months of not knowing if he was alive or dead, suffering or beyond suffering. Four months of Pierre asking questions she couldn't answer, of lying awake at night wondering if her father would live to see his grandchild.

"We do it," she said quietly. "But we do it my way, with my people, following my orders exactly. No heroics, no personal vendettas. We get in, we get our people out, we disappear. Anyone who can't follow those rules stays behind."

Pierre straightened, hope flaring in his eyes. "I can follow orders."

"Not yours." Marguerite met his gaze steadily. "You're staying with the reserve team, here in the mountains. If this goes wrong, if we don't come back, you're the new cell commander."

"Marguerite—"

Pierre stood suddenly, his chair scraping against stone. "I'm going with the assault team."

"Pierre—" Marguerite began.

"No." His voice carried a new authority, one that surprised even him. "I've listened to your tactical assessments, your casualty estimates, your contingency plans. You need every fighter you can get. Fifteen against twelve isn't enough—you said so yourself."

Marie watched this exchange with careful interest, her weathered hands folded on the table. Claude remained silent, but his eyes flicked between the siblings with something approaching approval.

"You're seventeen," Marguerite said, but her voice lacked its earlier conviction.

"The same age Papa was when he fought at Verdun." Pierre moved closer to the table, placing his hands flat against the rough wood. "The same age you were when you started carrying messages for the network. When did age become the measure of courage?"

Marguerite felt something shift inside her chest—pride mixed with terror, love complicated by the brutal arithmetic of war. "This isn't about courage. It's about experience."

"Then give me the chance to gain some." Pierre's voice softened, but his resolve remained firm. "I know these mountains better than most of your fighters. I can handle a rifle, move quietly, follow orders. What I can't do is sit here wondering if my father died while I was safely hidden in a cave."

The silence stretched between them, heavy with unspoken truths. Finally, Claude cleared his throat.

"Boy's got a point," the old fighter said gruffly. "We could use another gun, especially one that knows the terrain."

Marie nodded slowly. "And if we're asking parents to sacrifice their children for this war, perhaps we should let the children choose their own sacrifices."

Marguerite looked at her brother—really looked at him. Gone was the boy who had chased butterflies through lavender fields. In his place stood a young man who had already kept life-and-death secrets, who had seen friends disappear in the night, who carried the weight of their mother's hidden resistance work. The war had aged them all, but Pierre had grown into his responsibilities with a quiet strength that reminded her achingly of Henri.

"If you come," she said finally, "you follow orders without question. No heroics, no unnecessary risks. Your job is to get Papa out alive, not to prove anything to anyone."

Pierre's face lit up with fierce determination. "I understand."

"Do you?" Marguerite stepped closer to him, close enough to see the flecks of gold in his brown eyes, the slight tremor in his hands that betrayed his fear beneath the bravado. "Because if you die trying to save him, you'll destroy him anyway. Papa couldn't live with that guilt."

"Then I won't die." The words were simple, absolute, spoken with the confidence of youth that had not yet learned how little control anyone had over such things.

Marguerite felt her throat tighten. "Promise me."

"I promise." Pierre reached out and took her hand, his calloused palm warm against hers. "We both come home, Marguerite. All three of us."

Two days later, the pre-dawn air in the Maurel Pass was sharp with the scent of pine and cold stone. Hidden amongst the limestone cliffs, Marguerite's sixteen fighters waited, their breath pluming in the frigid air. The plan was a fragile thing, built on courage and desperation, and the silence stretched until it was a physical weight. Then came the low rumble of engines.

The German trucks labored up the winding road, just as their intelligence predicted. Marguerite gave the signal. The explosion that tore apart the road ahead was deafening, sending rock and debris showering down. Before the echo faded, Claude's team opened fire from the southern end, sealing the pass. The narrow ravine became a kill box of ricocheting bullets and shouted commands.

Marguerite saw Pierre beside her, no longer a boy playing at war, but a man forged in the crucible of this moment. His movements were economical and precise as he laid down cover fire, protecting the others as they advanced. The cost of the ambush was brutal and immediate. She saw Jean-Luc, a good man from the Lyon cell, fall in the first volley, a stark reminder that they were trading lives for a life.

The firefight was over in fifteen minutes of terrifying violence. "Now!" Marguerite yelled, and their people swarmed the trucks. Pierre was the first to the lead vehicle, wrenching open the doors. The prisoners inside were specters, gaunt and blinking in the sudden, harsh light.

"Papa!" Pierre cried out, his voice cracking with emotion.

Henri Dubois was there, his frame shockingly thin, but his eyes burned with an indomitable spirit. As Pierre helped him down, however, a deep, rattling cough seized him, and he leaned heavily on his son. He was alive, but the months in a German prison had seeded an illness that clung to his lungs. He looked from Pierre to Marguerite, his gaze a mixture of fierce pride and profound relief, before another fit of coughing wracked his body.

The journey back to the mountain camp was a somber procession. They had won. They had snatched Henri from the jaws of the Reich. But the victory was tainted by the fresh grief for the comrades they had lost. As Henri was settled into the infirmary cave, his shallow, labored breathing a constant, worrying presence, Marguerite understood that while one battle had been won, the war for her father's life was far from over. They had brought him home, but the prison, with its sickness and shadows, had come with him.

⚜

✺ 9 ✺

THE TRAITOR'S WEB

The coughing echoed through the limestone caverns like gunshots. Harsh. Wet. Persistent.

Marguerite pressed a damp cloth to her father's burning forehead, watching his chest labor with each breath. Six weeks since they'd pulled him from that German transport. Six weeks since Pierre had proven himself a man in the chaos of bullets and blood. Six weeks, and Henri was still fighting the infection that had taken hold in those filthy prison cells.

"The fever's stubborn," she whispered to Dr. Fournier, who knelt beside the makeshift bed. Her pregnancy showed clearly now—six months along, the child growing despite the meager rations and constant stress.

Fournier's weathered face remained concerned but not defeated. "Prison pneumonia. His body was weakened by months of poor conditions, but he's strong. The infection is deep, though—it will take time and care to clear completely."

"Will he recover?"

"His constitution is good. The rescue came before the worst

damage was done. But we must watch him carefully—this type of illness can turn dangerous quickly if we're not vigilant."

Around them, the mountain camp maintained its careful routines. Weapons cleaned. Sentries posted. Radio monitored. But underneath the discipline, Marguerite felt it—the creeping poison of suspicion. Three supply drops intercepted in two months. Too many patrols finding their camps. Too many close calls.

Someone was talking.

Pierre appeared at the cave entrance, rifle slung across his shoulders. At seventeen, he moved with the easy confidence of a seasoned fighter now. The rescue had changed him. The other men looked at him differently. Listened when he spoke. Henri's son, proven in blood.

"Marie wants to see you," he said quietly. "Something about the drop."

Another failed drop. Another betrayal.

Marguerite rose carefully, one hand supporting her back. The baby kicked—a strong, insistent movement that reminded her daily of James, somewhere in Scotland learning to kill. Learning to return to her.

"Watch Papa," she told Pierre. "If his breathing changes—"

"I'll find you." Pierre's voice carried new authority. The boy who'd once hidden behind her skirts was gone forever.

Marie waited in the operations cave, maps spread across rough tables, radio equipment humming in the corner. Her face had hardened over the winter months. Too many losses. Too many friends dead because someone couldn't keep secrets.

"Show me," Marguerite said without preamble.

Marie pointed to a mark on the map. "Last night's drop. Coordinates were perfect. Weather clear. But when our people arrived..." She gestured to a photograph. German soldiers. Waiting.

"How many knew the location?"

"Twelve." Marie's finger tapped names on a list. "Same twelve who knew about the Montpellier safe house. The Avignon contact. The arms cache near Marseille."

All compromised. All blown.

"One of our own." The words tasted like ash in Marguerite's mouth.

"Has to be." Marie lit a cigarette with shaking hands. "Question is which one."

Marguerite studied the names. Men and women she'd fought beside. Shared bread with. Trusted with her life. The thought that one of them—

"I have an idea." Marie's voice dropped to barely a whisper. "A trap."

Three hours later, Marguerite watched from the shadows as Marie briefed the cell leaders. Twelve people gathered around the radio, listening to fabricated coordinates for a fictional weapons drop. Each person given slightly different details. A test.

She memorized faces. Expressions. Who seemed nervous. Who asked too many questions. The weight of suspicion settled on her shoulders like a lead cloak.

Lucas Girard sat near the back. Twenty-two years old, joined the network six months ago after his village was burned. Quiet. Competent. Unremarkable.

But his hands trembled as he took notes.

Marguerite found Marie after the briefing, in the deeper caves where they stored ammunition. "Girard."

"You saw it too." Marie exhaled smoke toward the cavern ceiling. "The fear."

"Could be nerves. Could be—"

"Could be guilt." Marie crushed her cigarette against stone. "We'll know tomorrow."

The next evening brought news. German patrols surrounding the false coordinates. Girard's version of the location. Proof.

But confronting a traitor in a cave full of armed resistance fighters required delicate handling. One wrong word, one moment of panic, and the network could tear itself apart.

Marguerite approached Girard during the evening meal. He sat alone, picking at thin soup, staring at nothing.

"Walk with me," she said simply.

He looked up. Fear flickered in his eyes before he masked it. "Of course."

They moved through the camp slowly, her pregnancy making quick movement impossible anyway. Past the sleeping areas. Past the weapons cache. Into a smaller cave where acoustic quirks made conversation difficult to overhear.

"How are your sisters?" she asked conversationally.

Lucas went rigid. "What?"

"Your sisters. In Toulon. You mentioned them when you joined us. How are they?"

His face crumpled. The mask finally slipping. "They have them."

The words came out broken. Whispered. "Since November. Said they'd kill them if I didn't... if I couldn't..."

Marguerite felt her anger war with pity. "How much have you told them?"

"Everything." Lucas buried his face in his hands. "Every operation. Every safe house. I tried to give false information sometimes, but they knew. They always knew when I was lying."

"The Montpellier house. Sixteen people died."

"I know." His voice cracked. "I dream about them. Every night."

Marguerite studied the young man breaking apart before her. Two years ago, she might have felt only sympathy. But two years of war had taught her harder mathematics. Sixteen dead because one man couldn't sacrifice his family. How many more would die if they let this continue?

"What's your sisters' address?"

Hope flared in his eyes. "You'll help them?"

"I'll try." She wouldn't promise what she couldn't deliver. "But first, you're going to help us."

Marie joined them an hour later, along with Claude and three other senior fighters. Lucas sat in the center of their circle, confessing everything. Names. Dates. Methods of contact.

"We should shoot him," Claude said bluntly. "Quick. Clean. Send a message."

"To who?" Marie challenged. "The Germans already know we have a traitor. Killing him tells them we found their source."

"Better than letting him keep talking."

"But what if he didn't keep talking?" Marguerite interjected. "What if he started lying?"

The idea took shape as they discussed it. Use Lucas to feed false information. Let the Germans think their source remained intact while the network led them into traps.

Complex morality. The kind of choice that would have horrified her before the war.

"I'll do it," Lucas said quietly. "Whatever you want. I'll do it."

"You'll do it because the alternative is a bullet," Claude growled. "Don't pretend this is nobility."

"I know what it is." Lucas met their eyes without flinching. "I know what I am."

Later, after the others had gone, Marguerite sat alone with the radio equipment. A message had arrived through SOE channels. Coded. Brief. But the meaning clear enough.

James was coming home.

Spring deployment authorized. The Yorkshire rose returns to French soil.

She pressed her hand to her belly, feeling the baby's restless movement. James's child, growing strong despite everything. By the time he returned, she'd be nearing her final weeks. Heavy. Vulnerable. Hardly the efficient intelligence coordinator he'd left behind.

Pierre found her there, still staring at the decoded message.

"Good news?" he asked, settling beside her on the cave floor.

"James is coming back." She couldn't keep the mixture of joy and fear from her voice. "Spring."

Pierre nodded slowly. "About time. This baby needs a father."

"This baby needs a world worth living in." Marguerite folded the message carefully. "That's what we're all fighting for."

"Even Lucas?"

She considered the question. "Especially Lucas. He made terrible choices, but he made them for love. That's more human than monstrous."

"And now we're asking him to make different terrible choices."

"Yes." No point in pretending otherwise. "That's war. Everyone's hands get dirty eventually."

Through the cave entrance, she could hear her father coughing again. Henri, who'd survived German bullets and prison cells, brought low by something as simple as infected lungs. The irony wasn't lost on her.

Tomorrow, they'd send Lucas back to his German contacts with carefully crafted lies. False supply drops. Fictional safe houses. Information designed to waste German resources while protecting their real operations.

If it worked, they'd gain a precious advantage. If it failed...

If it failed, a lot more people would die.

But tonight, for just a moment, she allowed herself to imagine a different future. James returning to find her healthy, their child born safely, the war somehow ending with enough of them still alive to rebuild.

The baby kicked again, stronger this time. Demanding attention. Refusing to be ignored.

"All right," she whispered to the life growing inside her. "All right. I hear you."

Tomorrow would bring new betrayals, new tests of loyalty, new impossible choices. But tonight, she was still Marguerite Dubois, daughter of Henri, sister to Pierre, lover of James Crawford, mother of a child not yet born.

Still human, despite everything the war had demanded of her.

Still fighting for a future where that humanity might matter again.

The radio crackled in the corner, receiving another coded transmission. More orders. More operations. More chances to live or die for ideals that sometimes felt as fragile as lavender in winter.

But she listened anyway, decoded the message, began planning tomorrow's deceptions.

Because that's what resistance meant. Not grand gestures or heroic speeches, but the daily choice to continue fighting even when the enemy lived among you, even when trust became a luxury no one could afford, even when victory seemed as distant as the stars glimpsed through cave mouths on clear winter nights.

The war had changed them all. Made them harder, more suspicious, more willing to make compromises that would have seemed unthinkable before the first German jackboot crossed the French border.

But it hadn't broken them. Not yet.

And as long as they survived, as long as they kept fighting, there remained hope that something better might bloom from the ashes they were creating.

Even if none of them lived to see it.

☙❧

❧ 10 ❧

WINTER IN THE MOUNTAINS

WINTER 1942-1943

The cold was a living thing that crawled into their bones and refused to leave.

Marguerite pulled her thin coat tighter around her swollen belly and watched her breath form white clouds in the frigid air of the cave. Six months pregnant now, her body heavy and awkward, every movement requiring deliberate effort. Around her, the remnants of their resistance cell huddled around small fires that provided more psychological comfort than actual warmth.

Three weeks since the temperature had plummeted. Three weeks of gnawing hunger, dwindling supplies, and the constant fear that German patrols might find their high mountain refuge. The brutal cold was claiming lives, and morale grew thinner with each passing day.

But it was Henri's labored breathing that kept Marguerite awake at night.

"Papa?" She knelt beside his makeshift bed, pressing her hand to his forehead. The fever burned through his skin like fire. What had been a manageable infection just weeks ago had turned vicious, fed by the brutal cold and their meager rations.

Henri's eyes opened, glassy and unfocused. "Amélie?" he whispered, his voice paper-thin. "Is that you?"

Marguerite's throat tightened. He was seeing her mother. The infection was spreading, poisoning his mind as well as his lungs.

"It's Marguerite, Papa. I'm here."

His hand found hers, skeletal fingers gripping with surprising strength. "The baby..." he struggled to focus. "Is the baby safe?"

"Safe." She squeezed his hand gently. "Your grandchild is strong."

A ghost of a smile crossed Henri's cracked lips before another coughing fit seized him. This time, bright red blood splattered across the rough blanket. Too much blood.

Pierre appeared at her shoulder, his face grave. "How long does he have?"

Marguerite looked down at their father—the man who'd survived Verdun, who'd built a life from war-scarred earth, who'd taught them that some battles were worth dying for. His breathing was growing shallower by the hour, his skin taking on the waxy pallor she'd seen on too many faces in this cursed war.

"Not long. A day, maybe two." The words tasted like ash. "The cold is killing him as surely as any German bullet."

Through the cave mouth, wind howled like the voices of the dead. Snow had been falling for two days straight, sealing them into their mountain prison. At this altitude, even the hardiest resistance fighters struggled to survive. For a man weakened by months of imprisonment and fighting advanced pneumonia...

"We have to get him to Dr. Fournier," she said suddenly.

Pierre stared at her as if she'd suggested sprouting wings and flying. "Saint-Étienne is thirty kilometers away. Through mountain passes that are barely passable in good weather. You're seven months pregnant, and Papa can barely breathe."

"Then we'd better start now, before he gets worse."

"Marguerite—"

"He's going to die here!" The words exploded from her, echoing off the cave walls. Around them, other fighters looked up from their small fires, faces etched with the same desperate calculation she was making. "If we stay, he dies for certain. If we go..." She gestured helplessly at the white hell beyond their shelter. "At least there's a chance."

Pierre was quiet for a long moment, staring at Henri's deteriorating form. "I'll come with you."

"No." She struggled to her feet, one hand pressed against the small of her back. "Someone needs to protect the camp. If the Germans find this place while we're gone..."

She didn't need to spell out the massacre that would follow.

"Then take Claude. Or Marie."

"Marie is needed here to coordinate what's left of our network." Marguerite looked around at the faces watching them—too many old, too many young, too many weakened by hunger and cold. "But you're right about Claude. I can't manage Papa and the sledge alone in my condition."

The storm broke at dawn on the third day. Marguerite stood at the cave mouth, studying the treacherous landscape that stretched between them and Saint-Étienne. Thirty kilometers of knife-edge ridges, wind-scoured valleys, and snow that could swallow a person without trace.

Henri's breathing had grown so shallow that sometimes minutes passed between each labored breath.

"Take this." Marie pressed a small pistol into Marguerite's hands. "And this." A compass. "For God's sake, if the weather turns bad—"

"I know." Marguerite tucked the weapons into her coat. "If we're not back in a week, assume the worst."

Claude appeared with a makeshift sledge he'd constructed from pine branches and rope. "For him," he said gruffly, nodding toward Henri. "And I'm coming with you. You can't manage this alone."

The next hour was spent preparing Henri for transport. Extra blankets. Hot stones wrapped in cloth for warmth. A small supply of their precious medicine to keep him stable during the journey.

Pierre helped lift their father onto the crude sledge, his face carefully controlled. "Promise me you'll both be careful."

"I promise." She touched his face, seeing in his features the echo of Henri's stubborn courage. "Take care of everyone while we're gone."

"And if you don't come back?"

"Then you become the head of this family." She kissed his forehead the way their mother used to. "But we're coming back, Pierre. All three of us."

The first hour was a nightmare. The sledge caught on every rock, every root hidden beneath the snow. Henri's weight, even diminished by months of poor rations, made the going impossibly slow. Marguerite's enlarged belly threw off her balance, and Claude had to steady her more than once when she stumbled in the deep snow.

Henri drifted in and out of consciousness, sometimes calling for Amélie, sometimes murmuring orders to long-dead soldiers from Verdun. The fever dreams were getting worse.

By the second hour, even with Claude taking most of the sledge's weight, Marguerite was stopping every few minutes to catch her breath. The baby seemed to sense her distress, kicking and turning restlessly. Her back ached with every step, and the altitude was making her dizzy.

"Not yet," she whispered to her unborn child. "Hold on just a little longer."

The sun climbed higher but provided little warmth. Everything was white and glaring, a landscape scrubbed clean of color and mercy. Several times she lost the trail entirely, forced to backtrack and search for landmarks buried under fresh snow.

Halfway to Saint-Étienne, exhaustion forced her to rest in a shallow cave she remembered from childhood adventures. She built a small fire and tried to warm some broth for Henri, but he was too delirious to drink more than a few sips.

"Papa," she whispered, taking his burning hand. "Stay with me. Your grandchild needs to meet you."

His eyes opened briefly, focusing on her face with effort. "My brave girl," he breathed. "So brave..."

Then the fever took him again, and he was calling for dead comrades, giving orders to phantoms.

The afternoon brought new challenges. Clouds moved in from the west, threatening another storm. The temperature dropped further. Twice the sledge nearly went over hidden precipices where snow had accumulated over empty air.

But muscle memory guided her feet along paths her grandfather had shown her decades ago. Left at the lightning-split oak. Down the ridge where wild strawberries grew in summer. Past the rock formation that looked like a sleeping giant.

Saint-Étienne appeared in the distance just as the first new snowflakes began to fall. Henri had been unconscious for the last hour, his breathing so shallow that Marguerite had to press her ear to his chest to detect it.

Dr. Fournier's house sat on the edge of town, recognizable by the herb garden that remained green even under snow. Marguerite and Claude approached carefully, watching for signs of German occupation or surveillance. But the streets were empty, too cold for casual patrols.

Marguerite knocked on the back door—three short, two long, one short. The signal her mother had taught her years ago.

Fournier himself answered, his elderly face immediately creasing with alarm. "Mon Dieu, Marguerite! And Henri—quickly, bring him inside."

Together, the three of them managed to carry Henri into the warm kitchen. Fournier's medical instincts took over immediately, checking pulse, listening to labored breathing, examining the fevered eyes.

"Prison pneumonia," he confirmed grimly. "Advanced. How long has he been like this?"

"Three days getting worse. But the infection's been building for weeks."

Fournier was already moving, gathering supplies from his medical bag. "I have sulfanilamide powder, morphine for the pain. But he's very weak—too weak to survive another journey in this weather."

"Then we stay until he's stronger."

"There's a convent nearby," Fournier continued, preparing injections with practiced efficiency. "Sister Marguerite-Marie runs it. Good woman. She'll give you both sanctuary."

An hour later, Marguerite found herself in a small cell at the Convent of Saint Catherine, warmed by a brazier and wrapped in wool blankets that smelled of lavender. Henri lay in a nearby bed, breathing easier for the first time in days thanks to Fournier's medicines.

Sister Marguerite-Marie, a woman in her sixties with kind eyes and calloused hands, brought soup and bread that tasted like the food of heaven.

"Dr. Fournier explained your situation," the nun said, settling into a chair between the two beds. "You're both welcome here as long as necessary."

"Thank you, Sister. We won't impose long—"

"Your mother would be proud."

Marguerite looked up sharply. "You knew my mother?"

Sister Marguerite-Marie smiled. "Amélie Dubois was a remarkable woman. She helped us save many children during the early days of the occupation."

"Children?"

"Jewish children, mostly. Some refugees. Your mother would arrive in the middle of the night with little ones who needed new identities, safe passage, temporary homes." The nun's voice carried deep respect. "She never spoke of it, never sought recognition. She simply did what needed to be done."

Another layer of her mother's secret life revealed. Marguerite looked at Henri, sleeping peacefully for the first time in weeks, and wondered how many secrets their parents had carried.

"The Kellerman children," she said slowly. "Pierre told me she hid them in 1941."

"Among others. We have records, if you'd like to see them someday. Names, dates, where they went. Some made it to America. Others to Palestine. A few stayed in France with new families."

That night, Marguerite dreamed of her mother—not the woman weakened by illness that she remembered from those final months, but Amélie in her prime. Strong. Determined. Moving through darkness to save children whose names she would never speak aloud.

She woke before dawn to the sound of distant explosions.

Sister Marguerite-Marie appeared in the doorway, already dressed. "German attack on the mountains. Started two hours ago."

Marguerite's blood turned to ice. "My people—"

"Dr. Fournier is gathering supplies. If there are survivors, they'll need medical attention."

Henri was awake now, the fever finally broken, his eyes clear for the first time in days. "What's happening?"

"The Germans found our camp." Marguerite was already struggling out of bed, her heart hammering. "Pierre—"

"Your brother is strong," Henri said firmly, though she could see the fear in his eyes. "Smart. If anyone could lead an evacuation..."

Dr. Fournier examined Henri again the next morning, his weathered face grave. "The infection is clearing, yes, but he's still very weak. Those months in prison, the pneumonia—his body needs time to properly heal."

"How much time?" Marguerite asked, though she already dreaded the answer.

"Weeks. Maybe months. He needs warmth, proper food, constant care. Another journey through those mountains in his condition..." Fournier shook his head. "It would kill him."

Henri tried to protest from his bed. "My people need me—"

"Your people need you alive," Marguerite said firmly. "And right now, that means staying here."

"I won't abandon them."

"You're not abandoning anyone." She took his hand, feeling how frail it had become. "You're recovering so you can be strong for your grandchild."

After heated discussions with Dr. Fournier and the nuns, they reached an agreement. Henri would remain at the convent under medical supervision until his strength returned. Claude would return immediately to help Pierre coordinate the survivors. Marguerite would follow once Henri was stable, to assess the situation and coordinate the network's next moves.

"I don't like leaving you here," Claude said gruffly as he prepared for the return journey. "Not in your condition."

"I'll be safer here than in those caves," Marguerite assured him. "Tell Pierre that Papa is alive and recovering. And Claude—" She touched his arm. "Thank you. I couldn't have saved him without you."

The gruff fighter's face softened. "Your father is a good man. We don't abandon good men."

"I don't like this either," Henri said as Claude departed. "You, making that journey back alone, in your condition..."

"I made it down here. I can make it back." She kissed his forehead, noting with relief that the fever had completely broken. "Rest, Papa. Get strong. We'll need you in the spring."

The journey back up the mountain was brutal but mercifully solitary. Marguerite followed the smoke trails and her own tracks, her enlarged belly making every step an effort. But determination drove her forward—she had to find Pierre, had to know how many had survived.

She found them in caves so high and remote that her lungs burned with each breath. Eighteen ragged figures huddled around tiny fires, survivors of a massacre that had claimed too many friends.

Pierre met her at the cave entrance, his face cycling through relief, hope, and desperate worry. "Papa?"

"Alive. Safe. Recovering with Dr. Fournier." She embraced her brother, feeling how much weight he'd lost in just the few days since the attack. "He wanted to return with me, but he's too weak. The journey would have killed him."

Pierre nodded, understanding flooding his young features. "We lost twenty-nine confirmed dead. Seven missing, probably captured."

The numbers hit like physical blows. Friends. Comrades. People who had trusted her leadership and died while she was away saving one life.

"You did everything you could," she said, seeing the guilt written across his face. "You saved who you could save."

"Marcel. Simone. Dr. Mathieu." Pierre's voice cracked as he named the dead. "That first mortar round hit the main cave. We lost so many in the first minutes, before we could even react."

Marguerite closed her eyes, feeling the loss like a physical wound. She grieved for Dr. Mathieu, whose kindness had been a small light in the darkness. She grieved for Marcel and Simone, and for the two dozen others whose faces she now saw only in memory—friends and comrades lost in an instant.

"Who's leading now?"

"I am, I suppose." Pierre's voice carried new authority, forged in the crucible of command. "Sylvie handles communications, what little we can manage. Young Robert coordinates supply runs. But we're scattered, Marguerite. Barely functional."

Around them, the survivors went about the business of making another impossible shelter into something resembling home. They looked up when Marguerite passed, faces brightening at her return, at the news that Henri lived.

That night, as brother and sister sat by a small fire, Pierre finally allowed himself to show the full strain of command.

"I thought I'd lost both of you," he said quietly. "When the attack started, when I realized you weren't there to give orders, that it was all on me..."

"But you gave them anyway," Marguerite said proudly. "You led an evacuation under fire. You saved eighteen lives."

"We lost twenty-nine—"

"You saved eighteen." She echoed what Henri would have said. "In war, you count the lives saved, not the ones you couldn't reach. That's the only way to stay sane."

Pierre nodded slowly, accepting the harsh mathematics of resistance. Around them, the other survivors settled into their new reality —higher, colder, more isolated than they'd ever been.

But alive.

Outside their refuge, wind howled through peaks that scraped the sky. Below them, somewhere in the darkness, German patrols searched for the terrorists who had dared to resist their occupation.

Down in Saint-Étienne, Henri was safe under Dr. Fournier's care, slowly rebuilding his strength for whatever battles lay ahead.

Here, in this impossible mountain refuge, what remained of their cell prepared to endure another winter, another test of their determination to keep fighting.

Scattered. Broken. But unbeaten.

Still believing that love and courage could survive even in the coldest, most unforgiving places on earth.

છુજી

❧ II ❧
THE UNQUIET
CONVALESCENCE

FEBRUARY 1943

The peace of the Convent of Saint Catherine settled over Henri Dubois like morning mist—gentle, encompassing, yet suffocating in its very tenderness. For a man whose hands had known soil and steel, whose ears had grown attuned to the whisper of wind through lavender and the distant rumble of German trucks, the profound silence of the cloister felt like a slow drowning.

The first weeks blurred together in fever-dreams where sulfanilamide battled the infection in his lungs with all the determination of trench warfare. Dr. Fournier's precious medicine and the nuns' ceaseless ministrations pulled him back from the edge, but as clarity returned to his vision and strength seeped into his limbs like reluctant spring sap, the hallowed quiet began to scrape against his soul like fingernails on stone.

His days fell into the rhythm of bells—Lauds, Prime, Terce—each chime marking another hour his children spent hunted in the high places while he lay safe in pressed linens. He would walk the stone corridors, his Verdun limp tapping out a familiar morse code against ancient flagstones, while the soft susurrus of prayers in adjacent chambers reminded him of secrets he was no longer part of keeping.

Through tall windows, he watched winter sunlight trace skeletal patterns across walls that had sheltered centuries of souls seeking sanctuary. But sanctuary, he was beginning to understand, was a luxury the war had stolen from his family. Each shaft of light that warmed his face felt like a rebuke—he was healing while his world burned.

"You are mending well, Monsieur Dubois," Sister Marguerite-Marie murmured one gray afternoon, setting down a bowl of thick vegetable soup that steamed like incense in the cold air. Her kindness was as nourishing as the food itself, but it only sharpened the blade of his uselessness. "Your daughter's courage gave you life. You must honor that gift with patience."

Henri's fingers tightened around the wooden spoon, rough wood against callused palms. "My daughter faces wolves in the mountains, Sister. My son too. Every breath I draw in safety is one I steal from their struggle."

His voice, when he used it, had grown husky from weeks of disuse, but the words rang clear as chapel bells in the small cell. The nun's eyes —pale blue, wise with decades of comforting the afflicted—searched his face with the gentle persistence of water finding stone's weakness.

As February dragged its gray weight toward spring, Henri's restlessness crystallized into purpose. He chopped wood for the kitchen fires, the familiar rhythm of axe-fall and split kindling awakening muscles long dormant. Each swing tested his recovering strength, each impact a small rebellion against enforced peace. He mortared loose stones in the garden wall, his farmer's hands remembering the satisfaction of mending what weather had broken.

But with each task completed, each small victory over his weakened body, the mountains called to him with voices he recognized— Marguerite's fierce determination, Pierre's young courage, the whispered fears of fighters who had made themselves his family.

The catalyst arrived wearing travel-stained wool and exhaustion like a second skin. Father Benedict sought shelter for the night, his cassock dark with the mud of perilous roads and his eyes hollow with the weight of terrible news. Over thin soup by the kitchen fire, he spoke in hushed tones to the Mother Superior while Henri pretended to mend a leather harness nearby.

The Germans were tightening their grip on the hills with methodical brutality. Anti-partisan sweeps moved through the mountains like scythes through wheat. Near Grenoble, an entire network had vanished—not scattered, but erased completely. Betrayed from within, the priest whispered, his voice breaking like kindling.

Betrayed from within. The words lodged in Henri's chest like shrapnel. He saw Marguerite's face, drawn with exhaustion and responsibility she was too young to bear. Pierre's eyes, old before their time with the weight of secrets and survival. They were skilled, brave, resilient—but they were grieving, outnumbered, and stretched thin as wire.

They needed every experienced hand, every steady rifle, every scarred heart that understood the mathematics of loss and the algebra of hope.

That night, sleep eluded him as thoroughly as peace had. He lay on his narrow cot, staring at shadows that danced like phantoms across whitewashed walls, and made his decision with the quiet finality of a man who had already died once and found the experience wanting.

He could not be a passenger in his own life's final chapters.

Dawn came pale and silver through his small window, and Henri rose before the bell for Lauds. His few possessions—a loaf of bread, a small knife, the heavy woolen coat the sisters had provided—fit easily into a canvas sack. On the neatly made cot, he left a note written in his careful farmer's hand:

"Thank you for my life. I go now to defend my family's. May God protect you all."

The convent gate, which had welcomed him as a broken thing, opened now for a man reborn in purpose. He slipped through like smoke, leaving behind the peace he could not afford and embracing the war that would not release him.

The journey back into the mountains tested every ounce of strength Dr. Fournier's medicines had restored. Cold was a living enemy that clawed at exposed skin and turned each breath into visible proof of his mortality. The altitude seized his healing lungs with cruel fingers, but the skills learned in Verdun's mud had not abandoned him. He moved like a ghost through the landscape, reading terrain like scripture, following game trails and shepherd's paths that avoided roads and valleys where death might wait in field-gray uniforms.

For two days he climbed, descended, and climbed again, following instincts older than strategy and newer than hope. His body protested with every step, but his spirit lifted with each mile that brought him closer to the high places where his children waited.

He found them in caves that winter had scoured clean of all comfort—aeries of desperation carved into living rock. It was Pierre who spotted him first, his son's eyes widening with disbelief from his watchpost among the crags.

"*Papa?*" The word was torn from Pierre's throat and scattered by the wind.

Henri leaned heavily against a boulder, catching breath that seemed too thin for his needs, fighting dizziness that reminded him he was not yet the man he had once been. "Not a ghost, son. Just a stubborn old farmer who lost his way."

The reunion in the main cave was a tempest of relief and fury. Marguerite flew into his arms with the force of accumulated fear and love, her embrace fierce enough to crack ribs, but when she pulled back, her eyes blazed with protective fire he knew as well as his own heartbeat.

"What were you thinking?" she demanded, small fists planted on narrow hips in a gesture so precisely her mother's that his heart stumbled. "You were safe! You were healing! You were—"

"I was dying," Henri said quietly, his gaze sweeping over the gaunt, exhausted faces of the few survivors who looked to his daughter for salvation. "Not from pneumonia, *ma petite*. From being useless while my children fight my war."

He looked from Marguerite's worried face to Pierre's awestruck one, letting his love for them soften the steel in his voice. "I will not hide in holy places while my blood spills itself on these stones. My place is here. With my family. With my people."

The argument was brief because they all recognized the truth when it showed its face. Claude, the grizzled veteran whose scars told stories of a dozen battles, clasped Henri's shoulder with a grim smile that cracked his weathered features like spring ice.

"Welcome back, old man. We need your rifle."

And so Henri Dubois, who had been pulled from death's very threshold, returned to the war that had claimed him long before he understood the price of admission. He was no longer patient or invalid, but a fighter once more—his quiet strength and tactical wisdom a gift to the small, determined band who had made rebellion their religion.

His unquiet convalescence was over. His fight had never truly ended.

He was exactly where he needed to be when the betrayal that would shatter their world finally came.

⚜

12

THE SPRING OFFENSIVE

MARCH 1943

The first warm wind of spring carried more than the promise of melting snow—it carried the drone of aircraft engines overhead.

Marguerite stood at the mouth of their highest cave, one hand pressed against her swollen belly, watching three dark shapes descend beneath silk canopies against the star-scattered sky. Seven months pregnant now, her body heavy with child and hope, she felt her heart hammering as the parachutes drifted toward the predetermined landing zone in the valley below.

One of those shapes was James.

After seven months of coded BBC messages, of wondering if he was alive or dead, of carrying his child through the worst winter of her life—he was finally coming home.

"Marguerite." Pierre appeared beside her, no longer the romantic boy who'd dreamed of resistance glory, but a man hardened by command and loss. "Marie's teams are already moving to the drop zone. We should have confirmation within the hour."

She nodded, not trusting her voice. Around them, the remnants of their network stirred with new energy. The eighteen survivors who'd endured the German assault and the brutal winter were now part of something larger—a coordinated resistance cell that had grown from desperate refugees into an effective fighting force.

But it was the possibility of James's return that made her breath catch in her throat.

"The signals were correct?" she asked for the third time that evening.

"'The Yorkshire rose seeks its garden,'" Pierre recited the BBC code phrase. "'Tonight's moon illuminates the path home.' It's him, sister. It has to be."

The waiting was agony. Marguerite paced the cave as much as her condition allowed, while Pierre coordinated with their scattered look-outs. Since the winter attack, they'd restructured everything—multiple small camps instead of one large target, rotating leadership posts, redundant communication lines. They'd learned from their losses.

Marie appeared at the cave mouth just before dawn, her weathered face creased with something Marguerite hadn't seen in months: pure joy.

"Three agents confirmed. British SOE team, led by..." Marie's smile widened. "Flight Lieutenant James Crawford."

Marguerite's knees nearly buckled. Pierre caught her elbow, steadying her as tears blurred her vision.

"He's alive," she whispered. "He's really alive."

"More than alive," Marie continued. "He's been trained as a demolitions expert. Wireless operation. Weapons instruction. The SOE sent us a professional, Marguerite. This changes everything."

The reunion took place in a meadow carpeted with early wildflowers, where the sound of melting snow created a symphony of tiny waterfalls down the mountainside. Marguerite waited in the shadow of ancient pines, her heart threatening to burst from her chest.

When James emerged from the tree line, she barely recognized him. Seven months of SOE training had transformed the grateful, injured pilot into something harder, more dangerous. His face was leaner, his movements precise and controlled. Even his clothes—practical dark wool and leather—spoke of deadly competence.

But when his eyes found hers across the meadow, when he saw her swollen silhouette outlined against the morning light, everything professional about him crumbled.

"Marguerite." Her name was a prayer on his lips as he ran toward her.

She tried to run too, but her ungainly body managed only an awkward half-stumble before his arms closed around her. For a moment, the war disappeared. There was only James, solid and warm and alive, holding her as if he'd never let go again.

"I dreamed of this," he whispered against her hair. "Every night in Scotland, every day of training—I dreamed of finding you again."

"I wasn't sure you'd made it," she admitted, breathing in the familiar scent of him beneath the unfamiliar smell of British wool and military soap. "So many nights I thought—"

"I'm here." His hands framed her face, thumbs brushing away tears she hadn't realized were falling. "I'm here, and I'm never leaving you again."

It was then that he truly saw her condition. His gaze dropped to her belly, and his face went through a series of emotions so rapid and intense that she could barely track them: shock, fear, wonder, and finally, profound joy.

"A baby," he breathed, his hands trembling as they moved to her stomach. "You're carrying our baby."

"Seven months along," she confirmed, watching his expression carefully. "Conceived that last night before you left, before Marie took you to the network. James, I—"

"My God." His voice cracked as the magnitude hit him. "All this time, you've been carrying our child alone. Through the winter, through everything that happened—" He pressed his forehead against hers. "I should have been here."

"You're here now," she said firmly. "That's what matters."

For long moments they stood in the meadow, his hands spread across her belly, both of them marveling at the life growing between them. When the baby kicked, James's face lit up with such wonder that Marguerite felt her heart might break from happiness.

"Marry me," he said suddenly, urgently. "Here, now, today. I know it's not proper, I know we don't have papers or a church or—"

"Yes." The word escaped before he'd finished asking. "Yes, James Crawford. A thousand times yes."

Pierre, who'd been standing tactfully at the edge of the meadow with Marie and the other SOE agents, stepped forward with barely concealed delight.

"I think that can be arranged," he said, grinning. "Father Thomas at the monastery owes us several favors."

But Marie shook her head. "Too dangerous to move that many people to Séguret right now. German patrols have increased since the spring thaw." She studied the couple thoughtfully. "But there are other ways to make vows that matter."

That evening, as the sun set behind the jagged peaks, the survivors of their battered resistance cell gathered in a natural amphitheater of stone. Someone had found wild narcissus blooming in a sheltered crevice—the first flowers of spring. Claude, gruff as ever but surprisingly gentle, had woven them into a simple crown for Marguerite's hair.

Father Thomas had indeed come from the monastery, but so had twenty other fighters from cells throughout the region. Word had spread somehow—perhaps Marie's doing—that the British pilot who'd helped coordinate Allied supply drops was marrying the woman who'd saved him.

The ceremony was simple, conducted by moonlight with the priest's whispered Latin mixing with the sound of wind through pine boughs. Marguerite wore her cleanest dress, let out at the seams to accommodate her pregnancy. James wore his British uniform, the one reminder of the outside world beyond these mountains.

When they exchanged vows—promises spoken in both French and English, witnessed by men and women who'd seen too much death to take life lightly—Marguerite felt something shift inside her. Not just the baby moving, but something deeper. Hope, perhaps. The belief that they might actually survive this war, that they might have a future together.

"I take you as my wife," James said, his voice carrying clearly in the mountain air, "in war and in peace, in darkness and in light, until this madness ends and we can love freely again."

"I take you as my husband," Marguerite replied, her hands steady despite the enormity of the moment, "through whatever battles remain, through whatever losses come, until we can plant lavender together in a world at peace."

When they kissed, the assembled fighters erupted in quiet cheers —mindful even in celebration of the need for silence. Wine appeared from somewhere, saved for just such an occasion. Ancient songs were hummed rather than sung. For one night, the war seemed very far away.

But the war found them again the next morning.

James's SOE team brought more than just hope—they brought intelligence, wireless equipment, and most importantly, approval from London for the largest operation their network had ever attempted.

"Operation Hammer," James explained to the assembled leaders, unrolling maps on a flat stone that served as their conference table. "The Germans have been stockpiling munitions in an old limestone quarry fifteen kilometers northwest of Valensole. Artillery shells, small arms ammunition, explosives—enough to supply their defensive positions from here to Marseille."

Marie studied the topographical details, her experienced eyes tracing access routes and escape paths. "How do we know about this depot?"

"Allied reconnaissance," replied Agent Davies, James's demolitions specialist. "But also intelligence from your own network. A clerk at the mairie in Valensole—someone with access to transport manifests."

Marguerite felt a chill of recognition. That had been her intelligence, gathered during her time working at the town hall before her pregnancy became too obvious to hide. Information passed through dead drops and coded messages, now bearing fruit in ways she'd never imagined.

"The quarry's heavily guarded," James continued. "But the limestone formations provide natural cover for approach. If we coordinate simultaneous strikes—sabotage the access road, disable communications, hit the main depot—we can destroy months of German supply buildup."

Pierre leaned forward, his young face serious. "How many men would we need?"

"Forty fighters minimum. Divided into four teams." James's finger traced positions on the map. "Road team, communications team, perimeter team, and the demolitions crew."

"Forty." Marie whistled low. "That's nearly every fighter in the region."

"Which is exactly why it will work," Agent Phillips, the wireless operator, interjected. "The Germans expect small-scale harassment. They're not prepared for a coordinated assault of this magnitude."

For hours they planned, weighing risks against potential gains. The ammunition depot represented a strategic target that could cripple German defensive preparations for months. But the scale of the operation meant that failure would likely destroy their network entirely.

Marguerite listened to the tactical discussions with growing unease. Not because of the military plans—those seemed sound—but because of what the operation meant for her personally. At seven months pregnant, she could no longer participate in active missions. Her role would be limited to coordination and communications from a safe distance.

"I don't like leaving you behind," James said that night as they lay together in their small shelter, his hand resting protectively on her belly.

"I don't like being left behind," she admitted. "But I'm more useful alive than dead, and this little one needs at least one parent to survive the war."

"Both parents," James corrected firmly. "I didn't come back to you just to get myself killed in some quarry."

She turned in his arms, studying his face in the dim light of their small fire. "You're different. The training, the things you've learned—you're not the same man who crashed in our goat shed."

"No," he agreed quietly. "I'm not. The SOE doesn't just teach you to blow things up, Marguerite. They teach you to think like a soldier, to calculate acceptable losses, to make decisions that..." He paused, searching for words. "To make decisions that the man I was eight months ago never could have made."

"What kind of decisions?"

James was quiet for a long moment, his fingers tracing patterns on her shoulder. "When they drop you behind enemy lines, they tell you that your mission comes first. Always. Before friendship, before love, before your own life." His voice dropped to a whisper. "But they never told me what to do when the mission and the people you love become the same thing."

Marguerite understood. The operation against the quarry wasn't just about military strategy—it was about proving that their network could function as more than desperate survivors. It was about establishing their credentials for future Allied support. It was about building something that could outlast the war.

But it was also about forty people she cared about walking into the most dangerous mission they'd ever attempted.

"When do you leave?" she asked, though she already knew the answer from the maps and timetables she'd seen.

"Three days. The new moon gives us the best cover." James pulled her closer, his embrace tightening as if he could keep her safe through sheer force of will. "Marie's arranging for you to stay at the monastery while we're gone. Father Thomas has medical supplies if—"

"If the baby comes early," Marguerite finished. "I know. We've planned for everything except success."

"We'll succeed," James said with quiet conviction. "We have to. This war has taken too much from us already."

Outside their shelter, spring wind whispered through new leaves, carrying the scent of wildflowers and the promise of warmth to come. Somewhere in the darkness, sentries kept watch while wireless operators maintained contact with London. The network that had begun with a crashed pilot and a farmer's daughter had become something larger, more dangerous, more hopeful than either of them had ever imagined.

In three days, James would lead forty fighters against a German stronghold. In three months, if all went well, Marguerite would give birth to their child in a world slightly closer to freedom.

Tonight, they held each other in the mountains of Provence and dared to believe that love could survive anything the war might bring.

The baby kicked against her ribs as if in agreement, and Marguerite smiled in the darkness. Whatever came next, they would face it together—the family they'd chosen and the family they'd created, bound by promises made under starlight and sealed with hope stronger than fear.

13

THE BETRAYAL

The tension in the maquis camp had been building for weeks. Marguerite shifted uncomfortably on the wooden crate that served as her chair, her nine-month pregnant belly making every position awkward. Around the main cave, the other fighters moved with the careful efficiency of people who knew they were living on borrowed time.

"She's been feeding them information for months," Marie said, her voice carrying the cold precision that meant someone was about to die.

Madame Tessier sat with her hands bound, the baker's widow who had been providing safe houses since the beginning. Her round face, once so kind when offering bread to hungry fighters, now bore the hollow look of someone whose world had collapsed.

"The convoy routes," Pierre said from his position near the cave entrance. "The supply drops. All of it."

Marguerite watched the proceedings with growing unease. At nine months pregnant, she could no longer participate in operations the way she once had, and the enforced inactivity was a source of constant tension. The others treated her like fragile glass, while she felt useless, watching critical decisions being made without her input.

"They threatened my grandson," Madame Tessier whispered. "My daughter's boy. They said they would—"

"Enough," Marie cut her off. "How many of our people are dead because you chose one life over dozens?"

The sound of engines reached them before anyone could respond. Heavy trucks. Multiple vehicles climbing the mountain road with the systematic approach that meant only one thing.

"Everyone out," James commanded, his SOE training taking over. "Emergency evacuation. Now."

But the engines were already too close, and the systematic spread of sound through the forest below told them what they all dreaded— this wasn't a patrol. This was a coordinated assault.

For a heartbeat, Marie's hand trembled on her sidearm. Three years of working with this woman, of trusting her with their lives. Then her face hardened, the cold precision of a professional taking over. She drew her weapon and shot Madame Tessier through the heart. The sound echoed through the cave as chaos erupted around them.

"The quarry convoy," Pierre shouted over the growing noise. "They used our own operation as a diversion."

The first mortar shell struck the ridge above their position, sending a cascade of limestone and dirt down into the main cavern. Marguerite struggled to her feet, her swollen body unwieldy and slow.

"Henri!" she called, looking for her father near the radio equipment.

"Here!" Henri's voice came from deeper in the cave system where he was systematically destroying their communications gear with quick, practiced blows.

James appeared at Marguerite's side, grabbing their emergency pack. "Can you move?"

"I have to," she said, wincing as the baby kicked against her ribs.

The assault was massive and coordinated. Through the cave mouth, they could see German forces spreading through the forest with devastating efficiency. Not Wehrmacht—this had the systematic precision of SS troops.

"They know everything," Marie said, gathering intelligence files to destroy. "Every safe house, every contact, every route."

Another shell exploded, closer this time, and the concussion sent Marguerite stumbling. James caught her arm, steadying her.

"Emergency tunnels," he said. "Everyone to the emergency tunnels."

But as they moved toward the rear of the cave system, the sound of explosions came from those exits too. The Germans had surrounded them completely.

"How many ways out did they know about?" Pierre demanded, checking his rifle.

Marie's face went white. "All of them. They know about all of them."

The main entrance erupted in gunfire as German soldiers breached the outer defenses. The methodical chatter of machine guns mixed with the screams of their sentries being overrun.

Marguerite felt James's hand on her back, guiding her toward one of the secondary passages. The narrow tunnel that led to the eastern face was their last hope.

"Henri!" she called again, but couldn't see him through the smoke and chaos filling the cave.

"I can't see him," James said grimly. "We have to move."

"We can't leave him!"

"We don't have a choice!"

Pierre appeared from the smoke, blood running down his face from a head wound. "I saw Papa heading toward the north tunnel with Claude's group," he reported. "They must have gotten out ahead of us."

"Thank God," Marguerite said, relief flooding through her.

They stumbled through the emergency passage as the systematic destruction continued behind them. Three years of careful preparation, of building networks and gathering intelligence, being obliterated in minutes.

They emerged onto a narrow ledge overlooking the valley. Below them, the forest crawled with German soldiers. Trucks. Artillery pieces. This wasn't a raid—this was a military operation planned with devastating precision.

"My God," Marie breathed. "There are hundreds of them."

Pierre pointed to the convoy vehicles. "SS markings. Das Reich division."

The realization hit them all simultaneously. This wasn't just about destroying their cell—this was about destroying the entire regional network. Every safe house, every contact, every operation they had built over three years.

Marguerite pressed her hand to her belly, feeling the baby's agitated movements as her own heart raced. "Henri," she whispered, looking back at the smoke pouring from the cave system. "I hope he made it out with the others."

"Marguerite." Marie's voice was calm but urgent. "If Henri went out the north tunnel, he's ahead of us. We need to reach the secondary rendezvous point."

"You don't know he's dead!"

"He knows these mountains better than anyone," James said quietly. "If anyone can get out, it's Henri."

The sound of systematic searching rose from below. German voices calling coordinates. The methodical elimination of everything they had built.

"Where do we go?" Pierre asked, his young face aged by the horror of watching their world burn.

Marie checked her radio, trying to raise other cells, other safe houses. Static. Broken transmissions that cut off mid-sentence. The devastating scope of the betrayal became clear.

"Nowhere," she said finally. "They hit everything simultaneously. The whole network is blown."

Marguerite leaned against the rock face, one hand on her swollen belly, feeling utterly helpless. At nine months pregnant, she couldn't fight, couldn't run, could barely walk without assistance. She had become a liability at the moment when survival depended on speed and mobility.

"This is my fault," she said quietly. "I should never have stayed. I should have gone to Switzerland with the other women."

"Don't," James said fiercely. "Don't you dare blame yourself for their betrayal."

But Marguerite felt the weight of every decision, every operation she had planned while growing increasingly unable to execute them. The mounting pressure of the past weeks, the constant tension of knowing she was slowing them down, now seemed to have led inevitably to this catastrophe.

"We rebuild," Pierre said suddenly, his voice carrying a new hardness. "However many of us are left, wherever we can hide—we rebuild."

Marie looked at the three of them—a heavily pregnant woman, her teenage brother, and a British agent whose cover was now blown. The remnants of a network that had once spanned three departments.

"With what?" she asked. "Our people are dead. Our supplies are destroyed. Our safe houses are compromised."

Below them, the systematic destruction continued. Bodies of their comrades being dragged from the caves. The efficient, professional elimination of everything they had fought for.

But they were alive. Broken, scattered, reduced to almost nothing —but alive.

And sometimes, in war, survival was the only victory possible.

❧

❧ 14 ❧

THE LONGEST NIGHT

The pain came in waves now, relentless as the tide, each contraction gripping Marguerite's swollen belly with a force that drove the breath from her lungs. She pressed her back against the rough stone wall of the shepherd's hut, her fingers clawing at the ancient mortar between the stones as another surge of agony rolled through her.

"How long between them now?" Sylvie asked, her voice steady despite the circumstances that had brought them to this isolated refuge high in the mountains.

"Two minutes," Marguerite gasped, tasting blood where she had bitten her lip. "Maybe less."

It had been a month since the attack that destroyed their world. A month of hiding in caves and abandoned buildings, of moving constantly through the mountains while German patrols swept the valleys below. A month of watching their network crumble, their friends disappear one by one into the machinery of occupation and reprisal.

And now, in this primitive stone hut that had sheltered shepherds for centuries, her child was determined to be born.

"Good," Sylvie said, arranging the few supplies they had managed to gather. "That's good. Your body knows what to do."

Claude stood at the single window, his weathered face creased with worry as he scanned the treeline below. The veteran fighter had been with them since the evacuation, one of the few from their original cell to survive the betrayal. His rifle rested against his shoulder with the casual familiarity of a man who had carried weapons longer than some of their comrades had been alive.

"Still clear," he reported quietly. "But that patrol this morning came closer than I like."

Marguerite tried to focus on his words, on anything other than the building pressure in her body, but another contraction seized her and she couldn't suppress the low moan that escaped her throat. The sound echoed in the small space, primal and raw.

"Let it out," Sylvie said, moving to kneel beside her. "Don't fight it. Let your body do its work."

The hut was barely large enough for the three of them. Ancient stone walls blackened by centuries of smoke, a dirt floor covered with dried grass and sheep wool that Claude had gathered from the hillside. It smelled of animals and age and the lingering smoke from their small, carefully hidden fire.

Not where she had imagined bringing her first child into the world.

"James?" she whispered between contractions.

"Pierre went to find him at first light," Sylvie said, checking the water they had boiling in a dented pot over their meager fire. "They'll be here."

But Marguerite knew the reality of their situation. James and Pierre were three kilometers away, hidden in another refuge, maintaining the careful distance that was their only protection against detection. Even if Pierre had reached him, even if they were already making their way through the dangerous mountain paths, they might not arrive in time.

Her child was coming whether they were here or not.

Another wave of pain, stronger this time, and Marguerite felt something fundamental shift inside her body. A pressure, a tearing sensation that made her cry out despite her determination to stay quiet.

"That's it," Sylvie said, her hands gentle but certain as she examined Marguerite. "I can see the head. The baby's coming now."

Marguerite closed her eyes, feeling sweat run down her face despite the cool mountain air. In the distance, she could hear the sound of aircraft—German reconnaissance planes making their daily sweep of the region. The war continued around them, indifferent to the ancient drama playing out in this forgotten hut.

"On the next contraction, I need you to push," Sylvie said. "Push hard."

The pain built again, a crushing wave that seemed to split her in half, and Marguerite bore down with every fiber of strength she possessed. The world narrowed to this moment, this primal act of creation that transcended everything else—the war, the fear, the loss of everything they had built.

"Good, good," Sylvie murmured. "The head is out. One more push, Marguerite. One more and we'll have your baby."

Claude had moved away from the window, his face turned toward the wall in a gesture of privacy and respect. But his rifle remained ready, and Marguerite could see the tension in his shoulders as he listened for any sound that might indicate discovery.

The final contraction built slowly, then crashed over her like a breaking wave. She pushed with everything she had, feeling her body tear and stretch beyond endurance, and then suddenly the pressure released and there was a slippery, wet weight in Sylvie's hands.

For a heartbeat, the world was completely silent.

Then a thin, indignant cry pierced the air—the first sound of a new life entering a world at war.

"A girl," Sylvie whispered, her voice thick with emotion. "A beautiful, perfect girl."

Marguerite reached out with trembling hands as Sylvie cleaned the baby quickly with precious water and wrapped her in one of Marguerite's own shirts. The child was impossibly small, her skin red and wrinkled, her tiny fists waving in protest at being expelled from the warm safety of the womb.

"Hello, little one," Marguerite whispered, taking her daughter into her arms. The baby's cry subsided as she felt her mother's warmth, her unfocused eyes blinking in the dim light of the hut.

Marguerite looked down at her daughter's face and felt something break open in her chest—a love so fierce and immediate it was almost frightening. This tiny, helpless creature was hers. Flesh of her flesh, blood of her blood. A piece of the future they were all fighting to preserve.

"She's beautiful," Claude said quietly, his gruff voice gentle. "Looks like her mother."

The baby yawned, a tiny gesture that seemed impossibly perfect, and Marguerite felt tears running down her cheeks. After so much death, so much loss, here was life in its purest form. Hope made flesh.

"What will you call her?" Sylvie asked, cleaning up with efficient movements.

Marguerite looked at her daughter's serene face, thinking of all the names she and James had discussed during the long nights when the future had seemed more certain. But only one felt right now, in this moment, after everything they had endured.

"Espérance," she whispered. "Espérance Marie-Jeanne."

Hope. Named for the only thing they had left, and the only thing that mattered.

The sound of footsteps on the rocky path outside made them all freeze. Claude was at the window instantly, his rifle raised, but then his face relaxed.

"It's them," he said, and opened the door.

James and Pierre stumbled into the small space, both breathing hard from their climb through the mountains. James's eyes immediately found Marguerite and the baby, and his face transformed with an expression of wonder and joy so pure it took her breath away.

"Is she...?" he began, then stopped, overcome.

"Perfect," Marguerite said, holding out their daughter. "She's perfect."

James approached slowly, as if afraid he might break the spell, and took the baby into his arms with infinite care. The tiny child seemed impossibly fragile against his chest, her small head fitting perfectly in the palm of his large hand.

"Espérance," Marguerite said. "Espérance Marie-Jeanne."

"Hope," James whispered, understanding immediately. He looked up at Marguerite with tears in his eyes. "She's everything. She's absolutely everything."

Pierre moved to stand beside them, his young face soft with amazement as he looked down at his niece. "She's so small," he said quietly. "So perfect."

For a moment, the cramped stone hut was filled with a profound peace. The war seemed distant, the danger temporarily forgotten. There was only this—a new family, complete and whole, marveling at the miracle they had created.

But the peace couldn't last.

Claude had returned to his position at the window, and his posture had grown tense again. "We have a problem," he said quietly. "Patrol coming up the valley. Three vehicles."

James immediately handed the baby back to Marguerite, his protective instincts fully engaged. "How long?"

"Twenty minutes, maybe less. They're moving methodically, checking every structure."

Marguerite felt a cold fear wash over her. She had just given birth; her body was weak, exhausted, in no condition for another desperate flight through the mountains. But the approaching engines left them no choice.

"Can you travel?" James asked, his face creased with worry.

Marguerite tested her legs, struggling to stand. Pain shot through her lower body, and she had to grip Sylvie's arm for support. "I have to," she said simply.

"The monastery," Pierre said. "Séguret is only eight kilometers. If we can reach the brothers..."

"Eight kilometers through German patrols," Claude pointed out grimly. "With a woman who just gave birth and a newborn baby."

"Then we'd better move fast," James said, already gathering their few possessions.

Sylvie helped Marguerite to her feet, wrapping a blanket around her shoulders. Every movement sent waves of pain through her abused body, but she forced herself to ignore it. Espérance was depending on her now. They were all depending on each other.

"Can you carry her?" James asked, looking at the baby with desperate concern.

"Yes," Marguerite said, though she wasn't sure how long her strength would last. The adrenaline of the birth was fading, leaving behind a bone-deep exhaustion that threatened to overwhelm her.

Claude extinguished their fire and scattered the ashes while Pierre gathered the medical supplies. In minutes, they had erased all evidence of their presence in the hut.

The sound of engines was closer now, echoing off the valley walls below them.

"The old drovers' path," Claude said, shouldering his pack. "It's longer, but it stays on the ridgeline. Less chance of running into patrols."

They left the shepherd's hut in single file, Claude leading, then Marguerite with the baby, James close behind her, Pierre bringing up the rear. The night air was cool on Marguerite's fevered skin, and she shivered as they began their descent along the narrow mountain path.

Espérance slept against her chest, seemingly unaware of the danger surrounding them. Her small weight was both a comfort and a burden —proof of what they had to protect, and a reminder of how vulnerable they all were.

The path was treacherous in the darkness, barely wide enough for a single person, with steep drops on either side. Marguerite's legs shook with every step, and more than once James had to steady her when she stumbled.

"How much farther?" she whispered after what felt like hours.

"Halfway," Claude replied quietly. "You're doing well."

But Marguerite could feel her strength ebbing. The blood loss from the birth, combined with the physical demands of the mountain crossing, was taking its toll. Each step required enormous effort, and she could feel herself slowing despite her determination to keep pace.

Behind them, they could see the lights of the German patrol sweeping the valley, methodically checking each structure. The beam of their searchlights occasionally swept close enough to make them all freeze against the rocks until the danger passed.

"There," Pierre whispered, pointing ahead. "The monastery walls."

Through the darkness, Marguerite could make out the ancient stone walls of Séguret, silhouetted against the starlit sky. The monastery had stood in these mountains for eight hundred years, offering sanctuary to travelers and refugees. Tonight, it would shelter one more family fleeing the chaos of war.

Claude approached the heavy wooden gates and knocked softly—three short raps, two long ones, one short. An ancient code that the brothers had used for centuries to identify those seeking sanctuary.

The gate opened silently, revealing a robed figure holding a small lamp.

"Brother Augustine," Claude said quietly. "We seek sanctuary."

The monk's eyes took in their small group—the exhausted woman holding a newborn baby, the men with weapons, the desperate flight written in their faces.

"Come," he said simply, stepping aside to let them pass. "You are safe here."

They stumbled through the gates into the monastery courtyard, and Marguerite felt her legs finally give out. James caught her as she collapsed, Espérance still clutched safely in her arms.

"The child?" Brother Augustine asked, his voice full of concern.

"Born tonight," Marguerite whispered. "Born free."

The monk smiled, making the sign of the cross over the baby's head. "Then she is blessed indeed. Come, let us get you somewhere warm."

As they were led into the ancient stone corridors of the monastery, Marguerite looked down at her daughter's sleeping face. Espérance Marie-Jeanne—born in a shepherd's hut, carried through the mountains by moonlight, now safe within walls that had protected the innocent for centuries.

She was hope made flesh, proof that life would continue despite the war, despite the betrayals, despite all the darkness that had threatened to consume them.

The longest night was over. Her daughter had been born into freedom, and that was victory enough.

❦

❧ 15 ❧

THE RESCUE

JULY 1943

The stone walls of Séguret monastery held the coolness of centuries, but Marguerite felt sweat beading on her forehead as she paced the narrow cell that had become their refuge. Nearly two-month-old Espérance lay sleeping in a wooden cradle the brothers had carved for her, her tiny chest rising and falling with the peaceful rhythm of the innocent.

A soft knock at the door made Marguerite turn. Brother Augustine entered, his weathered face grave beneath his hood.

"There is news," he said quietly. "Marie is here with information about your father."

Marguerite's heart clenched. For two months, they had heard nothing of Henri's fate. The not knowing had been perhaps worse than certainty would have been—hope and despair warring constantly in her chest.

James appeared in the doorway behind the monk, his face tense with anticipation. "What news?"

Marie entered the small chamber, her clothes dusty from hard travel, her face bearing the lean look of someone who had been living rough in the mountains. In her hands she carried a folded paper that might have been torn from a German administrative document.

"He's alive," she said without preamble. "Henri is alive."

The words hit Marguerite like a physical blow. After so many weeks of fearing the worst, the simple fact of her father's survival seemed almost too much to absorb.

"Where?" James asked immediately, his SOE training taking over.

"Fort Saint-Nicolas. The old fortress overlooking Marseille harbor." Marie unfolded the paper, revealing what appeared to be a transport manifest. "This came from our contact in the administrative office. Your father's name is on a prisoner transfer list."

Marguerite took the document with trembling hands. There, in neat German script, she could see "Henri Dubois" among a list of twenty-three names. All scheduled for transport to Germany.

"When?" she whispered.

"Three days," Marie said grimly. "The convoy leaves at dawn on the fifteenth. After that..." She didn't need to finish. Everyone understood that prisoners sent to Germany rarely returned.

James was already studying the manifest, his mind working through possibilities. "The route?"

"Coastal road north from Marseille. They'll have to cross the Rhône at Arles—there's only one bridge the trucks can use. After that, they're on the main highway to Lyon."

Pierre had joined them now, along with Claude and the few other survivors of their network who had found sanctuary at the monastery. The cell felt crowded with their combined presence and the weight of what Marie was proposing.

"An ambush," Claude said, understanding immediately. "You're talking about an ambush on a German prisoner convoy."

"Twenty-three men," Marie confirmed. "Including Henri. All condemned to die in German labor camps if we do nothing."

Marguerite looked down at her sleeping daughter, then back at the transport list bearing her father's name. The choice seemed impossibly cruel—risk everything they had left for a desperate rescue attempt, or accept that Henri was already lost.

"It's suicide," Pierre said quietly. "A convoy that size will have escorts. Maybe a dozen SS guards, armored vehicles. We're three men with small arms."

"And we have the advantage of choosing the ground," James said, checking his rifle.

"James, no." Marguerite's voice was sharper than she intended. "I can't lose you too. Espérance can't lose her father."

He knelt beside the cradle, looking down at their daughter's peaceful face. "And she can't grow up never knowing her grandfather. Some risks are worth taking."

The debate continued through the morning, voices raised and lowered as they worked through the impossibilities and slim chances. Brother Augustine provided them with detailed maps of the coastal region, his monastery having sheltered travelers on these roads for centuries.

"Here," James said finally, pointing to a spot where the road curved through a narrow valley. "If we position ourselves on the ridge, we can control the entire route. Force them to stop, create confusion."

"And then what?" Marguerite demanded. "Even if you stop the convoy, even if you free the prisoners, how do you get away? The entire region will be swarming with German troops within hours."

"We scatter," Marie said simply. "Each man for himself. Some will make it, some won't. But at least they'll have a chance."

Marguerite felt the weight of decision settling on her shoulders. As the network's intelligence coordinator, the choice was ultimately hers to make. Risk everything for a desperate chance, or accept the loss and preserve what little they had left.

She looked again at her daughter, then at the manifest bearing her father's name.

"We do it," she said quietly. "We bring Papa home."

The next two days passed in a blur of preparation. James and Pierre scouted the ambush site, finding positions on the rocky hillside that overlooked the coastal road. Claude worked with the monastery's blacksmith to modify their few weapons, creating crude but effective explosives from materials at hand.

Marguerite remained at Séguret with Espérance, her role now that of coordinator rather than active participant. The physical reality of new motherhood kept her from the field, but her mind remained sharp, planning contingencies and escape routes for a mission that everyone understood was likely to be their last.

On the morning of the fifteenth, she stood in the monastery court-yard as the men prepared to leave. James checked his rifle one final time, his face set in the grim lines she had come to know so well.

"Bring him home," she said, placing her hand over his heart.

"I will," he promised, then kissed her forehead. "Take care of our daughter."

She watched them disappear into the pre-dawn darkness—three men against the German war machine, carrying nothing but determination and the desperate love of family.

The hours that followed were the longest of her life.

Marguerite paced the stone corridors, Espérance in her arms, listening for any sound that might bring news. Brother Augustine offered prayers in the chapel, his Latin words echoing off ancient stones. The other monks went about their daily routines with the practiced calm of men who had seen centuries of human conflict.

It was nearly noon when they heard the first distant rumble of explosions echoing across the valley.

"It's begun," Marie said quietly, having remained behind to coordi-nate communications.

The radio crackled with fragments of German transmissions—confused voices reporting an attack on the prisoner transport, requests for reinforcements, orders to seal off the region. Through the static and coded language, they could piece together fragments of what was happening.

The ambush had succeeded. The convoy was stopped. Prisoners were escaping into the countryside.

But there was no word of their men.

The afternoon stretched endlessly. More explosions in the distance, the drone of aircraft overhead as German reconnaissance flights swept the area. Radio traffic increased, indicating a massive search operation underway.

As evening approached, Marguerite stood at the monastery gates, Espérance sleeping against her shoulder, watching the road that wound up from the valley. Any moment, she told herself, any moment they would appear—James and Pierre and Claude, with Henri among them.

The sun was setting when she saw the first figure struggling up the mountain path.

It was Pierre, moving slowly, supporting another man who could barely walk. As they drew closer, Marguerite's heart leaped—the second figure was Henri, her father, alive but clearly weakened by his imprisonment.

She ran to meet them, careful not to jostle the baby, tears streaming down her face as she reached her father.

Henri looked older, thinner, his face bearing the gray pallor of a man who had endured months of captivity. But his eyes, when they focused on her, still held the spark she remembered.

"Marguerite," he whispered, his voice hoarse. "My daughter."

"Papa," she sobbed, embracing him as gently as she could. "You're home. You're safe."

Then Henri's gaze fell on the bundle in her arms, and his expression transformed with wonder.

"Is this...?"

"Your granddaughter," Marguerite said, carefully transferring Espérance to her grandfather's trembling arms. "Espérance Marie-Jeanne."

Henri looked down at the baby's sleeping face, and Marguerite saw tears running down his weathered cheeks. "She's beautiful," he whispered. "Perfect."

The baby stirred at the sound of a new voice, her unfocused eyes opening to gaze up at this stranger who held her with such reverence.

"Hello, little one," Henri said softly. "I'm your grand-père. I've waited so long to meet you."

"Where are the others?" Marguerite asked Pierre, though part of her already feared the answer.

Pierre's face was grim. "Claude didn't make it. German patrol caught him covering our withdrawal. And James..." He swallowed hard. "James stayed behind to hold them off. Last I saw, he was pinned down in the rocks above the road."

The joy of her father's return was immediately tempered by fresh terror. "Is he...?"

"I don't know," Pierre said honestly. "The shooting stopped about an hour ago, but that could mean anything."

Henri, still cradling his granddaughter, looked up with fierce concern. "He stayed behind? For us?"

"Yes, Papa. Espérance's father."

Henri's expression grew fierce despite his weakness. "Then he'll find a way back to you. A man doesn't abandon his family."

But the hours turned to days, and there was no word of James. German patrols swept the mountains, searching for the escaped prisoners and the men who had freed them. Henri grew stronger with rest and proper food, but he remained too weak for the rigors of mountain life.

"I'm a liability," he said on the third day, watching Marguerite pace with Espérance. "I'll slow you down if you have to run again."

Marie had been thinking the same thing. "There are people who can get you to Switzerland," she said carefully. "The brothers know routes through the mountains. You could recover there, wait out the war in safety."

Henri looked at his granddaughter, his face torn with conflict. "Leave her again, so soon after finding her?"

"Not forever," Marguerite said, though the words cost her. "Just until it's safe. Until the war is over."

It was Brother Augustine who settled the matter. "There is a convoy leaving tomorrow for the Swiss border," he said. "Refugees, wounded partisans, Jewish families seeking asylum. One more man will not be noticed."

Henri spent that evening holding Espérance, memorizing every detail of her tiny face. "When this war ends," he told her solemnly, "grand-père will come back and teach you about the lavender. About the land our family has worked for generations."

The baby seemed to listen, her solemn eyes fixed on his face as if understanding the gravity of his words.

On the eleventh day after the rescue, as Henri was preparing to leave for Switzerland, a figure appeared on the mountain path.

It was James, alive but clearly wounded, his left arm hanging useless at his side, his face gaunt with exhaustion and pain. He moved slowly, favoring his right leg, but he was walking under his own power.

Marguerite flew to him, Espérance in her arms, and he caught them both in his good arm, holding them with desperate strength.

"I thought I'd lost you," she whispered against his shoulder.

"Never," he said hoarsely. "I promised to come back, and I keep my promises."

Henri approached slowly, studying the man who had married his daughter and fathered his granddaughter. "You're James."

"Yes, sir. James Crawford."

Henri extended his hand, and James took it with his good arm. "Thank you," the older man said simply. "For bringing me home. For giving me the chance to meet her."

James looked down at Espérance, who was reaching up toward his face with tiny fingers. "Thank you for raising such an extraordinary daughter."

The reunion was complete, three generations united despite everything the war had thrown at them. But Henri still had to leave, still had to make the dangerous journey to Switzerland while his body recovered from the ordeal of imprisonment.

They said their goodbyes at dawn, Henri kissing his granddaughter's forehead one last time.

"Tell her about me," he said to Marguerite. "Tell her about the farm, about the lavender. Tell her that grand-père will be waiting for her when she's old enough to come home."

"I will, Papa. I promise."

As the convoy disappeared down the mountain road, carrying Henri toward safety, Marguerite stood with James and Espérance in the monastery courtyard. They had rescued her father, proven that love could triumph over the machinery of war, but the cost had been high.

Claude was dead. Their network was scattered. James was wounded and would need weeks to recover.

But they were alive. All of them, somehow, were alive.

And Espérance had met her grandfather, had felt his love and blessing before he disappeared again into the chaos of war.

It was enough. For now, it was enough.

🏵 16 🏵

THE ALLIED LANDING

AUGUST 1944

The dawn sky over the Mediterranean was painted in shades of steel and rose when Marguerite first saw the Allied armada. From her position on the coastal cliffs near Saint-Tropez, she counted more ships than she had ever imagined could exist in one place—battleships and destroyers, transport vessels and landing craft, stretching to the horizon like a vast metallic forest sprouting from the sea.

Operation Dragoon had begun.

"Mon Dieu," breathed Marie, crouched beside her with a pair of German binoculars they had liberated months earlier. "Look at them all."

Marguerite adjusted the radio pack on her shoulder and checked her watch. 0630 hours, August 15th, 1944. After fourteen months of careful rebuilding, of slowly reconstructing their shattered network, this was the moment they had been preparing for.

"Sector Seven reports all German observation posts neutralized," came Pierre's voice through her earpiece. Her brother had grown into a formidable saboteur, leading a team of fighters who moved through the coastal defenses like ghosts.

"Confirmed, Sector Seven," Marguerite replied, using the callsign that had replaced her name in all official communications. "Proceed to secondary targets."

Below them, the first landing craft were hitting the beaches. Even at this distance, she could see the tiny figures of Allied soldiers pouring onto French soil, finally bringing the liberation they had fought so long to achieve.

A year had transformed everything. The scattered, broken remnants of their network had grown into a sophisticated intelligence operation spanning three departments. Marguerite had rebuilt from the ashes of betrayal, creating new cells, new contacts, new methods of gathering and transmitting the information that was now proving crucial to the Allied advance.

But the greatest transformation was personal. Fourteen-month-old Espérance was no longer the helpless newborn who had entered the world in a shepherd's hut. She was a curious, determined toddler who had learned to walk among the ruins of occupied France, who spoke her first words to an extended family of fighters and refugees.

And now, for her safety, she was sixty kilometers away at the monastery of Séguret, where the brothers would protect her from the chaos of liberation.

"Marguerite." James's voice crackled through the radio from his position with the Allied liaison team. "We have contact with the beachhead. They're requesting immediate intelligence on German defensive positions inland."

"Stand by," she replied, then switched frequencies to contact her network of spotters positioned throughout the region. "All stations, this is Control. Report German positions and movements. Priority Alpha."

The responses came flooding in—a year's worth of careful observation and intelligence gathering condensed into crucial tactical information. German artillery positions disguised as farmhouses. Ammunition depots hidden in village cellars. Troop movements along interior roads.

The accumulated knowledge of a resistance network that had learned to see everything while remaining invisible.

She relayed the information to James with the practiced efficiency of a professional intelligence coordinator. The farm girl who had once calculated survival in terms of requisitioned livestock was gone, replaced by a woman who could coordinate multiple operations across hundreds of square kilometers while maintaining radio discipline under fire.

"Excellent work," came the reply from Allied command. "This intelligence is saving lives on the beaches."

From their clifftop position, Marguerite could see the effects of their preparation. Where German strongpoints should have commanded the landing zones, there was only silence—the fruits of Pierre's sabotage operations over the past month. Where enemy observers should have been directing artillery fire, the positions stood empty, their occupants eliminated by resistance fighters in pre-dawn raids.

"The Nineteenth Army is pulling back from the coast," reported one of her agents from a position near Toulon. "Large convoy moving north on the Route Nationale. At least two hundred vehicles."

Marguerite smiled grimly as she relayed this to the Allied air command. Within minutes, she could hear the drone of fighter-bombers moving inland to intercept the retreating Germans.

The morning progressed with the methodical precision of a plan years in the making. Each piece of intelligence her network provided found its way to Allied commanders, who used it to outmaneuver and outfight an enemy that suddenly found itself fighting blind.

But the work was not without cost. Radio traffic brought news of casualties among the resistance fighters—brave men and women who had emerged from the shadows to strike at German positions, only to find themselves in firefights they were not equipped to win.

"We've lost contact with the Sainte-Maxime cell," Marie reported grimly. "Last transmission indicated they were under heavy attack."

Marguerite felt the familiar weight of command—the knowledge that every order she gave might send someone to their death. But this was the price of liberation, the cost of the freedom that was finally, miraculously, within reach.

By midday, the Allied beachhead was secure. Thousands of soldiers had landed along the coast, bringing with them the overwhelming firepower that would drive the Germans from southern France. But Marguerite knew that the real work was just beginning.

"James, what's your status?" she asked over the radio.

"Moving inland with the advance elements," came his reply. "The Allies want liaison officers with local knowledge. I'll be attached to the First Armored Division."

James had transformed as much as she had over the past year. The crashed pilot who had once hidden in their goat shed was now a professional SOE agent, fluent in French, fully integrated with the resistance, and trusted by Allied command to coordinate between the regular forces and the irregular fighters who knew every stone and stream in these mountains.

"Be careful," she said, knowing he would understand the deeper meaning behind those simple words.

"Always am," he replied, and she could hear the smile in his voice despite the static.

The afternoon brought a different kind of chaos as the resistance emerged from the shadows to work openly with Allied forces. For three years, they had been ghosts, moving unseen through an occupied landscape. Now they were partners in liberation, and the adjustment was not always smooth.

Marguerite found herself mediating between American officers who wanted immediate action and French commanders who understood the complexity of the political landscape. There were jurisdictional disputes, communication breakdowns, and the inevitable friction that arose when regular military forces tried to integrate with irregular fighters who had their own methods and priorities.

"These resistance fighters," complained a colonel from the Forty-Fifth Infantry Division, "they don't follow proper military protocol."

"With respect, sir," Marguerite replied in English that had improved dramatically over the past year, "they have been following the only protocol that kept them alive for three years. Perhaps we could find a middle ground."

It was delicate work, requiring all the diplomatic skills she had developed as a network coordinator. But gradually, the two forces began to work together more effectively, the Allies providing the heavy firepower while the resistance fighters offered the local knowledge that no amount of map study could replace.

The week that followed was a blur of constant activity. Marguerite coordinated intelligence operations from a series of temporary command posts, moving closer to the coast as the Allied advance pushed inland. German resistance was crumbling faster than anyone had dared hope, but there were still pockets of fierce fighting as the enemy tried to establish defensive lines in the interior.

Pierre distinguished himself leading sabotage operations against German supply lines, his teams striking bridges and communication lines with the precision that came from intimate knowledge of the terrain. His reports crackled over the radio with the confidence of a seasoned military commander, and Marguerite felt a surge of pride in what her little brother had become.

Marie worked with the Allied intelligence services, helping to process the flood of information coming from resistance networks throughout the region. Her experience in coordinating multiple cells made her invaluable in managing the complex flow of tactical and strategic intelligence that was driving the rapid Allied advance.

But through it all, Marguerite found herself thinking of Espérance, safe but distant at Séguret. She had missed her daughter's first steps because of a sabotage operation, heard about her first words second-hand through a coded radio message. The cost of resistance work had always been personal, but it felt different now that she had a child.

On the seventh day after the landings, as German resistance finally collapsed completely along the coast, Marguerite received the message she had been waiting for.

"All clear," came James's voice over the radio. "The coast is secure. Time to go home."

She packed her radio equipment and intelligence files with hands that trembled slightly with exhaustion and relief. Seven days of nonstop operations had taken their toll, but they had succeeded beyond their wildest hopes. The Germans were in full retreat, and southern France was free.

The drive to Séguret took them through villages decked with tricolor flags, past cheering crowds who pressed flowers and wine on anyone in Allied uniform. The liberation was real, tangible, after so many years of occupation and oppression.

James met her at the monastery gates, looking older and more worn than when she had last seen him, but with a light in his eyes that had been absent for too long.

"How is she?" Marguerite asked before they even embraced.

"Perfect," he said, pulling her close. "Absolutely perfect. And asking for her maman every day."

They walked through the familiar corridors where they had taken refuge so many times over the past year. The monastery had become a second home, a place of sanctuary that had sheltered them through the darkest periods of their struggle.

Brother Augustine was waiting in the courtyard, and beside him was Espérance.

Marguerite's daughter had grown dramatically in the week they had been apart. She was toddling around the stone courtyard with the determined independence of a child who had learned early that the world was an uncertain place but was not to be feared.

"Maman!" Espérance called out when she saw Marguerite, running toward her with arms outstretched.

Marguerite dropped to her knees and caught her daughter in a fierce embrace, feeling the solid weight of her, breathing in the familiar scent of her hair. Seven days had felt like a lifetime, and the relief of holding her child again was overwhelming.

"Did you miss me, little one?" she whispered in French.

"Beaucoup," Espérance replied solemnly, one of the many words she had learned from her extended family of fighters and refugees.

James knelt beside them, completing the family circle. For a moment, they were just parents reunited with their child, their love a small but powerful flame in a world that had known too much darkness.

"The war isn't over," James said quietly, understanding that this moment of peace was temporary.

"No," Marguerite agreed, looking up at the monastery walls that had sheltered so many refugees over the centuries. "But we're winning. Finally, we're winning."

Espérance looked up at them both with the serious expression that had become characteristic of a child who had grown up among adults fighting for their lives. She was a product of occupied France, shaped by circumstances no child should have to endure, but she was also proof that life could persist and flourish even in the darkest times.

"Papa," she said to James, reaching up to touch his face with small fingers. "Home?"

James looked at Marguerite, and she saw in his eyes the same question that had been haunting her own thoughts. Where was home now? The farm where she had grown up was still occupied territory. Their life had been one of constant movement and danger for so long that the concept of a permanent home seemed almost foreign.

But as she held her daughter and felt James's arm around her shoulders, Marguerite realized that home wasn't a place. It was this—the three of them together, safe and whole, with the freedom to choose their own future.

The Allied landing had been a success beyond their wildest dreams. The resistance network she had built from the ashes of betrayal had proven its worth on the most important day in the history of occupied France. They had played their part in the liberation of their homeland.

Now they could begin to imagine what came next—a future where Espérance could grow up free, where the lavender fields of Provence might bloom again in peace, where the choice between survival and resistance would no longer define every waking moment.

The war wasn't over, but for the first time in years, it felt like it might actually end. And when it did, they would be ready to build something new from the ruins of everything they had lost.

❧

✣ 17 ✣

LIBERATION AND LAVENDER

SEPTEMBER 1944

The morning mist hung low over the Dubois farm when Marguerite first saw her childhood home after more than two years of exile. The old stone farmhouse stood exactly as she remembered it—weathered walls the color of honey, red tile roof softened by decades of Provençal sun, the ancient oak tree beside the kitchen door still spreading its protective canopy over the courtyard.

But it was the lavender fields that made her breath catch in her throat.

Row upon row of silver-green plants stretched across the hillside, their purple spikes catching the early light like scattered amethysts. Someone had tended them through the occupation, someone had preserved what three generations of Dubois hands had cultivated from this stubborn Mediterranean soil.

"Incroyable," James murmured beside her, shifting Espérance to his other arm. Their fifteen-month-old daughter was staring at the scene with the wide-eyed wonder of a child seeing magic for the first time.

"They're beautiful, Maman," Pierre said quietly, his voice thick with emotion. At twenty-one, her brother bore the weathered look of a man who had seen too much, but his eyes held the wonder of the boy who had once run through these very fields, chasing butterflies and dreams of heroism.

A figure emerged from the farmhouse—Madame Rousseau, their neighbor, moving slowly with the careful gait of someone in their seventies. She had been watching for them, Marguerite realized, waiting for their return with the patience of someone who understood that some journeys take longer than others.

"Marguerite, ma petite," the old woman called, opening her arms. "You've come home."

Marguerite ran to her, this woman who had been like a second mother throughout her childhood, and felt tears streaming down her cheeks as weathered arms embraced her.

"Madame Rousseau, how did you—? The fields, the house, everything is perfect."

"Did you think I would let the Germans destroy what your grand-mère built?" the old woman scolded gently. "Your family has been good to mine for forty years. It was my honor to watch over things until you returned."

She led them through the familiar rooms, pointing out small improvements and careful maintenance. The furniture had been protected with old sheets, the windows kept clean, the lavender harvest carefully dried and stored in the traditional wooden boxes that had belonged to Marguerite's grandmother.

"The distillery?" Marguerite asked, almost afraid to hope.

"Working perfectly. I had my nephew come twice a year to maintain the equipment. The Germans never bothered with it—they thought it was just an old woman's hobby."

In the kitchen, real coffee waited—precious coffee, the first Marguerite had tasted in over three years. They sat around the scarred wooden table where she had learned to read, where her mother had taught her to calculate household expenses, where her father had planned each season's planting with the methodical care of a man who understood that the land was both master and servant.

Espérance toddles around the kitchen with the fearless curiosity of a child discovering new territory. She pulled herself up on chair legs, investigated every corner, babbled in the mixture of French and English that had become her natural language.

"She has your mother's eyes," Madame Rousseau observed, watching Espérance with the indulgent smile reserved for the very young and the very old. "And your determination, I think."

"God help us all," James said with mock despair, but his eyes were soft as he watched his daughter explore her heritage.

They spent the morning walking the property, reacquainting themselves with every corner of the land that had shaped them. The lavender was indeed magnificent—testament to Madame Rousseau's care and the resilience of plants that had been bred for this harsh, beautiful landscape for centuries.

But it was when they reached the old distillery, with its copper pots and carefully maintained equipment, that Pierre finally spoke the words Marguerite had sensed building in him all morning.

"I need to tell you something," he said, his voice barely above a whisper. "Something I should have said long ago."

James and Marguerite exchanged glances. There had been secrets between them all during the war—necessary secrets, protective secrets, the kind of half-truths that kept people alive when truth itself had become dangerous.

"Early in the war," Pierre continued, staring at his hands, "when I was still seventeen and thought I knew everything about heroism and sacrifice, I did something terrible."

He told them about the approach—a German intelligence officer who had cultivated him carefully, exploiting his youth and his romantic notions about resistance work. How they had pressured him with threats against his family, how they had offered him money and protection in exchange for information.

"I gave them intelligence," he said, the words falling like stones into still water. "Minor things, misleading things, but still... I was feeding information to the enemy."

Marguerite felt her world tilt slightly, but she forced herself to listen without judgment. The boy who had made those choices was not the man standing before her now.

"What kind of information?" James asked, his SOE training making the question automatic.

"Patrol routes I'd already heard were changing. Supply drops that had been cancelled. The locations of abandoned safe houses we'd already evacuated." Pierre's voice grew stronger as he continued. "I made sure everything I gave them was either useless or actively helpful to our cause. But I was still collaborating, still betraying the trust you placed in me."

"Why?" Marguerite asked simply.

"Because I thought I could handle it. Because I thought I was clever enough to turn their own methods against them. And because..." His voice broke slightly. "Because I was terrified they would hurt you. Both of you. Everyone I loved."

The silence stretched between them, filled with the distant sound of bees working among the lavender blossoms and Espérance's happy babbling as she investigated a butterfly.

"How long?" James asked.

"Six months. Until the network was restructured after Madame Tessier's betrayal. Then I couldn't maintain the contact safely, and they lost interest in a source who wasn't providing useful intelligence."

Marguerite walked to the window that looked out over the lavender fields, thinking about the impossible choices they had all faced, the moral compromises that war demanded from everyone who lived through it.

"Did anyone die because of the information you gave them?" she asked finally.

"No. I made sure of that. Every piece of intelligence was carefully chosen to protect our people while seeming valuable to them."

"Then you weren't collaborating," James said firmly. "You were running a counter-intelligence operation. A dangerous, sophisticated operation that protected your network while feeding the enemy false information."

Pierre looked up, surprise evident in his face. "But I was only seventeen. I didn't know what I was doing."

"The hell you didn't," Marguerite said, turning back to face him. "You took an impossible situation and found a way to protect your family while serving the resistance. That's not betrayal, Pierre. That's courage."

She embraced her brother, feeling the last of the barriers between them dissolve. They had all made choices during the war—terrible, necessary choices that would have been unthinkable in peacetime. What mattered was not the compromises they had been forced to make, but the intentions that had guided them and the results they had achieved.

"We forgive you," she said simply. "Though there's nothing to forgive."

The afternoon was spent in the practical work of homecoming. They unpacked their few possessions, aired out rooms that had been closed for too long, began the careful inventory of what could be salvaged and what would need to be replaced.

But it was in the early evening, as the sun began to set over the lavender fields, that the real conversation began.

"What happens now?" James asked, sitting on the stone wall that separated the farmyard from the fields proper. Espérance sat on his lap, pointing at birds and offering her own commentary in the mixed language that seemed perfectly natural to her.

"We rebuild," Marguerite said simply. "The distillery, the farm, our lives. Everything."

"The war isn't over," Pierre pointed out. "There's still fighting in the north. The Germans haven't surrendered."

"No," she agreed. "But for us, here, the war is moving away. We can finally start thinking about the future instead of just surviving the present."

Pierre was quiet for a long moment, pulling absently at the lavender stems beside the wall. "I've been thinking about that. About the future."

"And?"

"I want to stay for the harvest. Help rebuild what we've lost, replant what needs replanting. But after that..." He paused, searching for the right words. "The new French government is going to need people with unusual experience. People who understand how networks function, how to coordinate between different groups with different priorities."

Marguerite studied her brother's face, seeing the man he had become through the crucible of war. The romantic boy who had dreamed of glorious resistance was gone, replaced by someone who understood the subtle complexities of rebuilding a shattered society.

"You want to help rebuild France," she said.

"I want to help rebuild something better than what we had before. Something that won't collapse the first time it's tested by crisis."

James nodded approvingly. "The Allies will need people like you. People who understand how things actually work on the ground, not just how they look on paper."

"What about you?" Pierre asked. "Will you stay?"

James looked at Marguerite, and she saw in his eyes the same question that had been haunting her own thoughts. What did they do now that the crisis that had brought them together was finally ending?

"I'm British," he said carefully. "My commission is with the SOE. When the war ends, I'll have responsibilities."

"But this is your daughter's home," Marguerite said quietly. "This is her heritage. The lavender fields her great-grandmother planted, the distillery her grandfather rebuilt after the last war. Espérance is French, James. This is where she belongs."

"And where I belong is with both of you," he said firmly. "My war is ending, Marguerite. But my life—our life—is just beginning."

They sat in comfortable silence as the sun completed its descent toward the horizon, painting the lavender fields in shades of gold and purple that took Marguerite's breath away. This was the scene she had carried in her memory through all the dark months of exile—this particular quality of light, this specific arrangement of color and shadow that could only exist here, in this place, at this time of day.

Espérance had fallen asleep in James's arms, one small hand curled around his finger, her face peaceful in the way that only children could achieve. She was growing up between languages and cultures, shaped by circumstances that would have been unimaginable to her grandparents, but she was also rooted in this soil, connected to this land by bonds deeper than nationality or politics.

"She'll grow up free," Marguerite said softly. "Whatever else happens, she'll grow up in a free France."

"She'll grow up knowing she comes from people who fought for that freedom," Pierre added. "People who were willing to sacrifice everything to ensure she could have choices they never had."

As the first stars appeared in the darkening sky, they made their way back to the farmhouse. The kitchen glowed with warm light from the oil lamps Madame Rousseau had kept in perfect working order. The familiar smells of home—lavender and wood smoke and the lingering traces of a hundred years of family meals—wrapped around them like an embrace.

Marguerite tucked Espérance into the wooden cradle that had been her own bed as an infant, the same cradle that had held three generations of Dubois children. Her daughter stirred slightly at the familiar French lullaby Marguerite sang, the same song her own mother had sung to her in this very room.

Later, as James and Pierre discussed the practical details of rebuilding—which fields needed replanting, which equipment required repair, which markets might be available for their lavender oil—Marguerite stepped out into the courtyard one more time.

The night air was soft and warm, carrying the fragrance of lavender and the distant sound of night birds calling across the valley. Above her, the stars wheeled in their ancient patterns, the same stars that had watched over this land through conquest and liberation, occupation and freedom.

Tomorrow there would be work—the hard, patient labor of rebuilding a life from the fragments left by war. There would be practical decisions about crops and equipment and markets. There would be the slow process of healing wounds that went deeper than the physical.

But tonight, for the first time in more than three years, Marguerite was home.

The lavender was blooming again, silver-green and purple under the starlight, beautiful and resilient and eternal. Her family was safe and whole and together. The future stretched ahead of them, uncertain but full of possibility.

As she stood in the courtyard where she had played as a child, where she had learned to walk and talk and dream, Marguerite felt something settle into place in her chest—a peace she had almost forgotten was possible, a sense of completion that made her understand why they had fought so hard to preserve this life, this place, this simple but profound gift of home.

The war would end soon. The lavender would continue to bloom. Her daughter would grow up in freedom, rooted in the soil her ancestors had tended for generations but free to choose her own path into whatever future awaited.

It was enough. After everything they had endured, everything they had lost and found and fought to preserve, it was more than enough.

It was everything.

⚛

EPILOGUE: WHEN LAVENDER
BLOOMS AGAIN

JULY 1962

The morning mist lifted from the lavender fields like a blessing, revealing row upon row of purple blooms that stretched across the hillside in perfect formation. Nineteen-year-old Espérance Marie-Jeanne Crawford moved through them with the easy grace of someone born to this rhythm, her grandmother's serpe catching the early light as she cut the fragrant stems with practiced precision.

"Not too low, ma chérie," called Henri from the next row, his voice still carrying authority despite his seventy-five years. The grandfather who had once been missing, presumed dead, now moved more slowly through the lavender, but his love for this work—and for his grand-daughter—remained undiminished.

Espérance smiled at the familiar reminder. "I know, Grand-père. Leave enough stem for next year's growth."

It was the same instruction her great-great-grandmother had given, passed down through four generations of women who had learned that lavender, like hope, required patience and faith in tomorrow. The ancient wisdom felt particularly meaningful this morning, as Espérance prepared to share news that would change everything and nothing at all.

Marguerite emerged from the farmhouse carrying the same blue enamel coffee pot that had served the family for more than twenty years, her forty-four-year-old face serene with the contentment of a woman who had found her way home. Behind her came James, silver threading through his brown hair now, walking with the quiet confidence of a man who had discovered that belonging was not about where you were born, but where you chose to build your life.

"Rest," Marguerite called, settling the tray on the stone wall exactly as her father had done during that last peaceful harvest in 1940. "The lavender isn't going anywhere."

Pierre appeared from the distillery, wiping his hands on a towel, his face bearing the satisfied expression of a man who had spent the morning coaxing perfect essential oil from the copper equipment their family had maintained for decades. At thirty-seven, he moved with the assured competence of someone who had found his calling—six months working with the new government had been enough to convince him that his heart belonged here, in these fields, continuing work that connected him to something larger than politics or ambition.

"The new distillation is perfect," he announced, settling onto the wall beside his father. "The oil is as clear and fragrant as any we've ever produced."

"Better," Henri corrected with satisfaction. "The new plantings James suggested have improved the quality significantly. Your mother would be amazed at what we've accomplished."

They always spoke of Amélie as if she had just stepped out of the room rather than died eighteen years ago. Her presence lingered in the carefully maintained school garden, in the French poetry Espérance recited by heart, in the quiet strength that had carried them all through the darkest years of the war.

Espérance accepted her cup of coffee—real coffee, available again for more than a decade but still appreciated by those who remembered its absence—and gathered her courage for the announcement she had been planning all week.

"I have news," she said, her voice carrying the slight accent that marked her as a child of two languages and two cultures. "About university."

Marguerite's hand stilled on her coffee cup. They had known this moment was coming—Espérance was brilliant, destined for larger things than the lavender fields could provide, no matter how much she loved them.

"The Sorbonne?" James asked gently.

"No, Papa. Cambridge. They've accepted me for modern languages. I want to study translation, interpretation. I want to help people understand each other across borders."

The silence that followed was filled with the drone of bees working among the lavender blossoms and the distant sound of church bells marking the hour from the village below.

"England," Henri said finally, and Espérance heard in his voice not disappointment but wonder at the paths that had led them all to this moment.

"Not forever," she said quickly. "Never forever. This is my home, these fields, this family. But I want to learn about the world beyond these hills. I want to understand how to prevent what happened to us from happening to others."

Marguerite set down her coffee cup and drew her daughter close, breathing in the scent of lavender that always clung to her hair. "You sound exactly like your father when I first met him—determined to save the world through sheer force of will."

"Did it work?" Espérance asked with a smile.

"Eventually," James said, his English accent still faint but unmistakable after all these years. "Though I suspect the world saved us as much as we saved it."

Pierre cleared his throat. "There's something else," he said, his face taking on the slightly embarrassed expression he wore when making announcements. "Sylvie has agreed to marry me."

This news prompted a genuine celebration—Sylvie Moreau had been courting Pierre for nearly two years, ever since they'd met at the regional agricultural cooperative where she worked as an accountant. At thirty-two, she was practical, kind, and had immediately understood why Pierre chose the lavender fields over the complexities of government work.

"When?" Marguerite asked, already planning the celebration and looking forward to welcoming this wonderful woman into their family.

"September, after the harvest. We want to wait until the work is finished, until we can celebrate properly without worrying about the timing."

Henri raised his coffee cup in an impromptu toast. "To the future," he said simply. "To all the futures we fought to make possible."

They drank to that—to Espérance's studies and Pierre's marriage and the continued prosperity of the farm that had anchored them all through the storms of the century. To Henri's return from Switzerland, fulfilling the promise he had made to his granddaughter when she was barely old enough to understand. To James's transformation from a crashed pilot to a Frenchman by choice and love. To Marguerite's journey from intelligence coordinator back to farmer, mother, and keeper of the family's memories.

The morning stretched ahead of them, filled with the familiar work of harvest that connected them to the land and to each other. But now it felt different—not like an ending or a continuation, but like a fulfillment of promises made during the darkest hours of the war.

"The east field needs finishing," Henri said finally, rising with the careful movement of a man who had earned his aches through decades of honest work. "But first, Espérance should tell us more about this Cambridge."

As they walked back toward the lavender rows, Espérance found herself memorizing the scene—the way the morning light fell across her mother's graying hair, the sound of her grandfather's laughter as her father told some elaborate story about British university customs, the comfortable weight of family tradition balanced against the excitement of future possibilities.

This was what they had fought for during the war—not just the right to survival, but the right to choose. The right for a young woman to study languages at Cambridge while knowing she could always come home to lavender fields that would bloom again, season after season, generation after generation.

The scent of lavender filled the warming air, carrying with it the essence of everything they had preserved and everything they had built from the ashes of destruction. Sweet and clean and eternal, it connected them to the past and promised them the future—a future where children could grow up free to choose their own paths while remaining rooted in the love and sacrifice of those who came before.

In her basket, the purple stems released their fragrance into the morning breeze, and Espérance smiled, understanding finally why her family spoke of lavender as if it were a living promise. It would bloom again next year, and the year after that, and for all the years her own children and grandchildren would work these fields.

Some things endured. Some things were worth preserving. Some things, once planted with love and tended with patience, bloomed again and again, no matter what storms might come.

The war was over. The lavender was blooming. The future was theirs to shape.

And in the distance, the church bells of their village rang out across the valley, calling the faithful to celebrate another day of peace in a world that had learned, once again, the true value of freedom.

❦

ABOUT THE AUTHOR

Eva Lyndale is a historical fiction author and lifelong explorer whose curiosity has carried her to more than forty countries. Her writing blends meticulous historical research with vivid storytelling, offering readers a window into distant eras and the lives shaped within them

From crumbling coastal ruins to bustling cities layered with centuries of change, the places Eva visits often spark the settings for her novels. She is especially drawn to overlooked moments in history—those quiet, human stories that unfold in the shadows of larger events. Through richly drawn characters and immersive environments, her work explores themes of connection, transformation, and the passage of time

Eva approaches each project with the mind of a researcher and the heart of a traveler, weaving cultural detail and atmospheric depth into every page. When she's not writing, she can often be found exploring local archives, wandering through museums, or sketching story notes in a tucked-away café somewhere new.

Printed in Dunstable, United Kingdom

66768981R00097